## "Pull up and cool off!

"You barged in here with your horse whisperer tricks, thinking you know more about horses than anyone."

"I don't think I know more than anyone else," Lyssa said calmly.

"Just mind your own business, will you?"

"Parker, that's enough!" Sam called.

Parker twisted in his saddle to see Sam come up behind him, her face like a thundercloud.

"Nerves are no excuse for this sort of rudeness. You owe Lyssa an apology," she commanded sternly.

"*I* should apologize? But—," Parker began.

Lyssa began to laugh, and Parker glared at her once more. Her musical laugh set Parker off more than anything else about her. "Don't worry about it, Sam. No offense taken," she said. And with that, she trotted off.

Gritting his teeth, Parker turned Foxy in the opposite direction. He'd show Lyssa what he thought of her and her advice. Squeezing his legs, he urged Foxy into a gallop and turned her toward the water jump.

"Parker, don't make things worse. Pull up and cool off!" Sam ordered. "I mean it. Slow down, Parker!"

# THOROUGHBRED

# CLOSE
# CALL

CREATED BY
## JOANNA CAMPBELL

WRITTEN BY
## KARLE DICKERSON

**HarperEntertainment**
*An Imprint of HarperCollinsPublishers*

HarperEntertainment
*An Imprint of* HarperCollins*Publishers*
10 East 53rd Street, New York, NY 10022-5299

Produced by 17th Street Productions,
an Alloy Online, Inc. company

HarperCollins books are available at special quantity discounts for bulk
purchases for sales promotions, premiums, or fund-raising.
For information, please call or write:
Special Markets Department, HarperCollins Publishers,
10 East 53rd Street, New York, NY 10022-5299.
Telephone: (212) 207-7528. Fax: (212) 207-7222.

ISBN 0-06-106635-4

Cover art © 2000 by 17th Street Productions,
an Alloy Online, Inc. company

First printing: June 2000

Printed in the United States of America

Visit HarperEntertainment on the World Wide Web at
www.harpercollins.com

❖ 10 9 8 7 6 5 4 3 2 1

*To Joan Childs,*
*eventing instructor par excellence*

# CLOSE CALL

"NOT NOW! PLEASE, WAIT JUST A LITTLE LONGER!" PLEADED eighteen-year-old Parker Townsend as the gray skies rumbled over the expansive grounds at the Thorndale Horse Trial near Lexington, Kentucky.

But just then the clouds let loose, and fat raindrops began pelting his face.

*Great*, thought Parker. It *would* have to start raining right when he was about to enter the arena for his dressage test, the first phase of the trial.

"Not to worry, girl," he said calmly to his elegant bay Thoroughbred mare, Foxglove. "We've both been in worse weather. Kentucky rains are nothing compared to English rains."

Foxy tossed her head and snorted, as if remembering her days spent as a foal in England, her snaffle bit jingling lightly. Parker ran his white-gloved hand over her tightly braided mane while he rode her out of the schooling area. Then he smiled at himself. Who was he kidding? Foxy wasn't the one that needed soothing. She was a seasoned event horse who would need more than a little rain to rattle her. Parker had spoken more to calm himself.

After all, this was another big step toward his dream. Over the next two days he'd know whether he could continue to pursue his Olympic dream—or whether he'd be left in the dust. It didn't matter how badly he wanted to be chosen for the Olympic combined training team or how many previous three-day events he and Foxy had won. They had to place high in the ribbons today at Thorndale as well as at Deer Springs, a three-day event next month, for the selectors to consider them.

A one-day horse trial like Thorndale was a lot different than a three-day event. It had twenty-five cross-country obstacles instead of thirty-six and no roads-and-tracks phases or steeplechase. But many top-notch competitors used the Thorndale trial to fine-tune their horses for Deer Springs, and it took a very advanced level of riding to win it.

"Good luck," Parker's girlfriend, Christina Reese, called as she came up behind him. She and Parker had been dating for a couple of years, and Parker still couldn't believe his luck. She was a year younger than him and the daughter of racing legend Ashleigh Griffen, the first woman to win the Kentucky Derby and Preakness on her horse Ashleigh's Wonder. As an apprentice jockey, Christina was following in her mother's footsteps and already had several wins under her belt. Plus as far as Parker was concerned, Christina was a great girlfriend.

"You two look so perfect," Christina added, her strawberry blond hair plastered down from the rain. Her hazel eyes scanned over Parker quickly, obviously double-checking that he hadn't missed anything. Regulations at advanced-level trials like these were so rigid, one tiny detail could cause a rider to be disqualified. "You need anything?"

It was amazing—even though Christina was busy becoming a top-notch jockey, she still found time to help him braid and watch his test. Out of habit, Parker almost slipped into the accent he'd acquired during his English boarding school days and made a joke, but he changed his mind. "Thanks, Chris," he replied. "I think I've got it under control."

"You're lucky you got an early draw. The footing in the arena should still be decent," Christina said, wiping some mud from Parker's polished black dressage boots.

Parker shrugged and urged Foxy forward toward

the dressage ring. He never let anyone see how nervous he was. He had to stay focused.

Christina trotted alongside Foxy, keeping up a steady stream of chatter. Usually Parker was the one making the jokes and telling stories, but he knew that Christina was trying to keep him calm.

The rain was now drumming down steadily. Parker glanced into the stands and saw that despite the miserable weather, the crowd hadn't thinned out at all. People had come from miles away to see their favorite world-class riders. All the big-name event riders were competing—Cammie Dillon, Oliver Flores, Dave Breen, and Gillian Montgomery. Did he and Foxy really have a chance at being short-listed for the Olympics in such company?

"Hey, Townsend, rock the house," called Dave as he sloshed past, leading his rangy chestnut gelding. Dave's mud-covered boots stood out in contrast to his neatly pressed black shadbelly jacket, which he'd covered with a clear plastic raincoat.

Christina let out a low whistle. "Yikes, he's here, too? Didn't he win everything at Badminton?" she murmured, referring to the world-famous three-day event in England. She and Parker had watched the video several times to prepare for this trial.

Parker nodded and raised his whip at Dave. Then his eyes found their way to the bleachers. Luckily he couldn't see his parents anywhere in the stands. Normally they stayed away from Parker's events, but the local newspapers had made a huge to-do about this trial, and Parker had the feeling they just might turn up. He wished they wouldn't. Lavinia and Brad Townsend had made it clear that he'd let them down by pursuing eventing instead of the family business—breeding and training racehorses.

"Absolute nonsense," Brad had said with a sneer on more than one occasion.

"Eventing?" sniffed Lavinia. "But Parker, it's so . . . *common.*"

Over the years Parker had clashed with his opinionated and manipulative parents about so many things. First it had been their attempt to send him to school in England, where he'd "meet the right sort of people." He'd gotten kicked out for sneaking off campus to his uncle's racing stable. When Parker finally graduated from high school in Lexington, Brad wanted him to go to a business university in Italy. But Parker enrolled at the University of Kentucky so he could continue his riding career and be near Christina.

Parker wasn't the only one the Townsends tried to control. They also owned half of Ashleigh's Wonder and shared ownership of all her offspring with Christina's parents. Wonder had died two years before, so Wonder's Star was the last of the line. Ever since he was orphaned as a foal, Brad and Lavinia were forever interfering with Star's training and questioning the way Ashleigh and Christina handled him. Eventually Parker had had enough. After a heated argument he'd moved out of Townsend Acres and gone to live at Whisperwood Farm, where he worked and trained with Samantha Nelson and her husband, Tor.

But after a while Parker decided to move back home and give his parents another chance. This time he'd moved into a room in the west wing of the house, near the servants' quarters, where he'd be less likely to run into Brad and Lavinia. But they still managed to berate him for choosing eventing over racing, for not having his own groom to wait on him and Foxy, and for dating Christina, among other things.

*If only I could stand up to them once and for all,* he thought.

But now was not the time. He was about to ride one of the most important dressage tests of his life. Shaking his head to clear his thoughts, Parker walked Foxglove on a loose rein, watching the competitor before him finish up her test. As she saluted the judges and rode out of the arena, Parker collected Foxy and circled her. When the bell sounded, he urged the mare into a working canter and headed toward the entrance at the letter *A*. This was it.

"Wait, Parker," hissed Christina from behind him.

"Your whip. Drop your whip!"

Parker felt his heart pound as he dropped the long dressage whip. He couldn't believe it. He'd nearly disqualified himself before he'd gotten started!

*Cool it. Don't let anything distract you*, Parker thought fleetingly. He and Foxy executed a perfect halt at the X and saluted the judges. Parker cued the mare into a working trot, and they tracked to the left. Around the perimeter of the ring the crowd was deafeningly silent, as if it was holding its collective breath. Parker steered Foxy down the center line. Time for a shoulder-in.

*Good girl*, Parker thought as they completed this difficult move and tracked to the right. They changed rein, and invisibly Parker encouraged Foxy forward with his hands, legs, and seat. She responded by moving out in an extended trot, her hooves rapping out a steady beat from letter to letter in accordance with the test.

*Perfect, absolutely perfect*, Parker thought. Now the half pass, an advanced move at the walk requiring the horse to move on two parallel tracks, flexed slightly in the direction of the movement but with a straight spine. Then they made the transition to the working trot and, from there, the walk.

*Keep her balanced*, Parker told himself as he closed his hands on the rain-slicked reins. He settled deeper into his seat to bring Foxy up from behind.

It was while they were tracking to the left that Parker felt something wasn't quite right. Foxy's hindquarters weren't fully engaged. It was subtle, but still, the impulsion from behind wasn't what it should be. Willing himself not to frown, he gave Foxy a little outside leg at the letter *V* and closed his hands on the reins for the working canter. She brought her hind end underneath her as they circled at a canter, and moving from *F* to *S*, they changed rein with a flying lead change as soon as they hit the rail.

*Excellent*, Parker thought. Foxy was totally balanced now, and the flying change had been exact. He cantered Foxy up the center line and halted squarely, took off his top hat, and saluted the judge.

The pair trotted out of the arena, and the stands exploded in applause. Parker felt the tension lift, and he leaned over Foxy, hugging her neck. They were both soaked through with a mix of rain and sweat, but Parker didn't care.

"Good girl!" he crooned as they made their way toward the stabling area. Not a perfect test, he knew. But close enough. Dressage had never been his favorite discipline—he much preferred the fast pace and huge fences of cross-country. But he knew they would have to work on their dressage if they wanted to reach the Olympics.

Sliding off Foxy, Parker ran up the stirrup irons and

loosened the girth. He pulled off his shadbelly and threw it over the dressage saddle. Not that there was much point—the saddle was already soaked.

"Not bad," came a voice from right behind him. Parker turned to see a tall girl, about sixteen years old, wrapped in a turquoise horse cooler. She rubbed the tiny white star on Foxy's forehead. "What a gorgeous horse you are. You had a good test, too." Then, looking up at Parker with sky blue eyes, she added, "But that canter transition was sorta sticky, wasn't it?"

"What?" Parker demanded, startled. Was it that noticeable? Maybe he hadn't done as well as he'd thought he had. Parker looked closely at the girl. He didn't recognize her, but under the cooler he could see she was wearing a full dressage habit. Parker knew almost everyone on the eventing circuit, so he was surprised that she didn't look familiar. Parker blushed as he became aware of the girl's intense blue eyes staring back at him.

Suddenly Foxy pulled away from him and nuzzled the girl. Ordinarily Foxy wasn't very affectionate toward strangers.

*Maybe she has a mint in her pocket*, Parker mused. Ever since Parker's grandfather, Clay Townsend, had bought Foxglove for Parker at an auction, Parker had discovered that Foxy was crazy about mints, especially Polos, the English mints that his grandfather sent over from England specially for her.

"Well, see you around," the girl said. She patted Foxy's slick muzzle and then disappeared into the crowd swarming the show grounds.

Suddenly Parker felt a vague sense of annoyance at the strange girl. What right did she have to comment on his performance, anyway? Who did she think she was, his instructor? That would definitely come as a surprise to Sam, who was meeting him at Foxglove's stall so she could help him change his tack for the cross-country course and go over his ride fence by fence.

"Come on, Foxy, never mind her," Parker mumbled as he threw a cotton sweat sheet over the mare's back. Foxy shook her head, sending droplets of foam flying. It was then that Parker realized the rain had stopped.

*Good*, he thought. The twenty-five-jump cross-country course was demanding enough without being knee-deep in mud.

When they reached Foxy's stall, Parker untacked her and began to rub her steaming coat with a thick towel. Then he let her roll and rest for a few minutes while he sat down on her tack box and closed his eyes. Mentally he reviewed the cross-country course he'd walked twice—once yesterday and once early that morning. Horses weren't allowed to see the course beforehand, but Parker knew he needn't worry. Foxy loved to jump.

Ten minutes later Sam emerged from the trailer they were using for a tack room, carrying Parker's eventing saddle, overgirth, and bridle. Her red hair was caught up in a French braid, and she was wearing worn jeans and a sweatshirt. She looked more like a teenager than a woman in her late twenties.

"Great test," Sam said as she set the saddle down on the portable saddle rack. She glanced at her watch. "We'll talk more about that canter transition later. Right now you'd better get a move on and change. You're scheduled to start in forty-five minutes. I'll pull out Foxy's braids and tack up."

Parker smiled gratefully and ducked into the tack room, where he shed his formal dressage attire and pulled on his short-sleeved yellow shirt, safety vest, and cross-country helmet with its green-and-gold hat cover—Whisperwood's colors. Hastily grabbing his number pinny and the armband containing his medical information (just in case he had a bad fall), he opened the door and stepped outside. Samantha had just finished undoing Foxy's braids, and her black mane curled and frizzled.

"Bad-hair day, huh, girl?" Parker joked, reaching over to stroke her neck and slip her a Polo mint. Foxy crunched on her mint and nudged his hand, looking for more.

While Samantha finished tacking up Foxy, Parker

fastened on her bell boots, which would keep her hind feet from striking her front feet, and galloping boots to protect her legs.

"All set," Samantha said. "Now go get 'em. Remember to pace yourself and keep an eye out for slick spots. She might peek at Catherine's Cabana, so keep your leg on her." Sam was referring to an elaborate fence that looked like a surfer shack with a palm-covered roof and a bar area with little bar stools in front of it.

"Gotcha," Parker said, adjusting his armband and grinning. If there was anything he liked, it was a challenging jump.

He felt a shiver of excitement as he mounted and checked his equipment. He couldn't wait to get out there.

"Hey—awesome test," Christina called, and hurried over to Foxy's side. "Everyone in the stands is predicting that you're going to win this, you know," she said as they continued walking to the warm-up area.

Parker grinned. "What about that canter transition at *V*?"

Christina looked puzzled. "I didn't see anything."

Shrugging, Parker gathered his rubber reins. "Well, some girl noticed it. I guess she thinks it's her business to tell people what she thinks of their rides."

12

"What do you care about what people think? If I listened to every bit of criticism I heard about the way I ride Star . . ."

Parker knew Christina was referring to his parents. They were constantly appearing unannounced with their stopwatches to clock Christina's works at White-brook, the breeding and training farm where Christina and Star lived. Now that they were prepping Star for the Kentucky Derby, the Townsends were more relent-less with their criticism than ever.

"I know," Parker agreed. "But the way she said it, it was like she knew something I didn't."

"Weird," Christina said absently. "Well, I hear some Olympic selection people are here, so why don't you forget about what anyone says? You can win this, Parker!"

Parker smiled at Christina's encouragement and took up the reins. Since this was a trial and not a three-day event, there was no steeplechase phase to get horse and rider's blood pumping. Parker had to make his warm-up count if he was going to ride aggressively and avoid time penalties. Entering the gate to the warm-up area, he circled at a trot, then a canter, and steered Foxy over a low vertical fence. He could feel her gather herself as she jumped wide, tossing her head in a playful buck as she landed.

Parker shook his head and closed his hands on the

reins. "Get it out of your system now," he said. "No funny stuff on course."

Foxy settled down at the sound of his voice, and they flew over a low oxer. She was ready to work, responding instantly when Parker gave her a half halt to balance her before the next fence.

"Easy, now, Soldier Blue," a voice rang out as Parker brought Foxy back to a trot.

Parker turned his head to see the same dark-haired girl with the sky blue eyes ride into the warm-up area. She was wearing a black shirt and a turquoise safety vest and was mounted on a gangly flea-bitten gray.

*What an ugly horse!* Parker thought, gaping. He was about seventeen hands, with a huge head, floppy ears, and hooves the size of dinner plates. Then Parker noticed something else. The girl was riding the lanky gray without a bridle or saddle! Startled, Parker continued to stare.

Riding toward them, the girl gave Parker a friendly smile.

"We meet again," she said. Without waiting for a reply she turned her attention back to her horse, mumbling lovingly into his ear.

*The stewards will never let her compete like that*, Parker thought. "Uh, aren't you missing something?" he called out.

The girl flashed him a puzzled glance.

14

"Where's your tack?"

The girl tossed her head. "Oh, we don't use it. Old Blue knows what to do."

Parker stared openly as the girl trotted the gray toward a large chicken coop with a four-foot ground spread. Surely she wasn't going to jump such a big fence without a saddle or bridle. Parker's jaw dropped as she did just that—perfectly.

## 2

"HEADS UP!"

Parker couldn't believe what he'd just witnessed.

"Uh—hell-*oh*, Townsend! Could you please move so Blue and I don't make road pizza out of you?"

Parker squeezed Foxy's sides and scooted out of the way as the girl circled and galloped toward the round-top fence he'd been standing in front of.

"Where we come from, 'heads up' means you get out of the way," she called as she landed smoothly on the other side of the fence.

Parker glared. "It means the same thing here," he muttered under his breath. His eyes narrowed as he took in the strange rider's bright turquoise helmet cover and her horse's purple wraps. He was reminded of the wild Kool-Aid colors that Christina's cousin,

Melanie Graham, used to dye her hair before she decided to stick to being blond. And what was with the giant silver buckle sticking out from under the girl's safety vest? She looked like she was in the circus or something. Yet clearly she was about to ride the cross-country course.

They weren't going to let her out of the starting box without a bit in her horse's mouth, though. "Read any rule books lately?" he cracked, feeling mean as he said it, but there was no way the girl could have heard him from halfway across the ring.

Still, he couldn't take his eyes off the strange pair. Parker had to admit that the ugly gray could definitely jump! He folded his gangly legs neatly under his chest and cleared each fence with feet to spare. And though she had nothing but the gelding's bare back and mane to cling to, the girl followed her mount's movements effortlessly, never losing her balance and keeping perfect control.

*How does she do that?* Parker wondered as he cantered Foxy over their last two warm-up fences. He forced his thoughts back to his own warm-up and tried to stay out of the girl's way in case she suddenly lost control. *Actually she ought to be given a warning for being so reckless. Who does she think she is, anyway?*

It was only when Parker rode past her on his way to his last fence that he saw what he hadn't seen before.

Around the gray horse's neck was a wire. Every so often the girl would place her hand on the wire and move almost imperceptibly, sending signals to the gray.

"Hey, Lyssa," called a voice. "Only a few minutes left. Better get a move on."

Parker saw a tall, weather-beaten man wearing faded jeans, a denim jacket, and a crumpled straw cowboy hat walk over and raise the first vertical that the girl had jumped.

*So that's her name. Lyssa.*

"Aw, c'mon, Cal," Parker heard the girl say with a light, musical laugh. "Is that all? Blue could walk over that."

"Number seventy-nine, two minutes. Two minutes, number seventy-nine," crackled the voice over the PA system.

"That's us," Parker said, turning his attention back to his mare. He gathered his reins and trotted out of the warm-up area. Foxy knew she was about to gallop over five miles of challenging jumps, and she tossed her head and snorted excitedly.

"Take it easy, girl," Parker murmured, patting her damp neck. "Save your energy. We're going to blow them away."

Foxy danced sideways, eyeing a paper napkin lying on the ground. Parker sat deeper in his saddle,

18

closed his hands on the reins, and urged Foxy forward. When he reached the starting box, he glanced at the second hand on his watch and circled Foxy outside. He didn't want to enter the box a second before he had to—it would only get Foxy more jazzed.

"Ten, nine, eight . . ."

Parker and Foxy entered the starting box, keeping their backs to the opening in case Foxy exploded out of the box too early, disqualifying them. Parker's mouth was dry, his heart pounded in his chest. The second before the official shouted, *"Go!"* he wheeled Foxy around and pressed the stopwatch button on his watch.

Foxy lurched forward, and they galloped toward the first fence. The wind whipped Parker's face, and salty tears streamed down his cheeks. He leaned forward as they made their approach to the solid ascending ramp, counting down the strides in his head. Foxy brought her weight back in preparation for the takeoff and jumped roundly with room to spare.

"Good girl," Parker cried as they landed evenly on the other side.

Foxy galloped eagerly across the field, her nostrils flared in excitement. Adrenaline surged through Parker as they turned for the next fence. Foxy took it perfectly, slowing slightly when Parker checked her with a half halt. He didn't want any time penalties, but he didn't want Foxy to rush the fences, either. The next fence was big and set up on an angle. They'd need to be incredibly accurate. Five, four, three, two, one . . . Foxy sailed through the air, over the high side of the jump, landed in stride, and kept on galloping. They flew up a hill and through the narrow fence called the Picture Frame because the horse jumped through an opening in the center. Parker was vaguely aware of the spectators and the judges posted at every fence, but his eyes never strayed from the course. Foxy was performing brilliantly, taking each fence easily, eager for the next one.

"You're the best, Foxy," Parker whispered after a tricky trakehner fence. Parker had ridden the line absolutely straight, just the way he'd envisioned it when he'd walked the course earlier. It was a shorter route, demanding absolute accuracy, and Foxy had delivered.

*We saved a few seconds there!* Parker thought exultantly. He stood up in the irons, crouching low over Foxy's withers as they swept up the grassy track. Sam would think he'd cut it close, but she'd have taken the same bold route herself. Parker had seen enough videos of her eventing days in Ireland to know.

They came to the first of the water jumps, and Parker straightened himself in the saddle. Out of the corner of his eye he could see the throng of spectators.

The crowd tended to gather by these more dangerous water complexes, where the spills tended to be more spectacular.

*Sorry to disappoint you, but no way are Foxy and I going to fall.*

Earlier in his eventing career Parker had been a little more reckless, taking fences with alarming speed—and without considering the consequences. Once Parker had even jumped a huge preliminary-level fence when he was riding intermediate. Foxy had bobbled, and both she and her rider were seriously injured. During their slow recovery Parker had grown up a lot.

He was still bold, but he never took a fence without considering Foxy's safety. Now he approached the water with caution, but just the right amount of forward motion to give Foxy courage. The sun had just broken through for the first time that day, and the light playing on the water could be very distracting to her if he didn't communicate effectively. Parker closed his legs, offering his mount support and encouragement. He felt Foxy's powerful effort as she jumped down the steep bank into the water and kept charging through, water fanning out on both sides until she sailed up onto dry land again.

They continued on, galloping up a hill and turning sharply toward a brush jump. Here Parker could relax slightly, knowing Foxy was aware that the top wasn't solid and that she could brush it slightly without knocking it. One after another they met the fences in stride, sailing on to the seventeenth jump, Catherine's Cabana. Parker sat back and drove Foxy forward, keeping his gaze focused on the field on the other side of the jump. But Foxy didn't bat an eye and jumped the fence as if she'd been doing it for years. Parker checked his stopwatch and saw that they were well within the time limit. He could afford to bring Foxy back a little and take the next few jumps with even more precision.

Before he knew it, they were hurtling toward the last fence. Parker could barely contain his exhilaration. The last few months of training had really paid off. Foxy was one amazing horse, he thought triumphantly, never mind the best friend a guy could have!

Within seconds the two shot past the finishing flags. Parker wanted to let loose with a whoop. Instead he glanced at his stopwatch—no time penalties. Then he sat back in the saddle and began to slow her, rubbing her sweat-soaked neck.

Gradually they came down to a walk, Parker's blood still pumping wildly through his veins. "You're the best," Parker whispered, leaning low over Foxy's neck. Her ears flicked back and forth. He smiled as he heard the announcer's voice: "No faults for number seventy-nine, Parker Townsend and Foxglove!" and the clapping that ensued.

Parker barely heard the congratulations from other riders and spectators as he slid off and loosened the girth. He mumbled his thanks to the compliments as he made his way back to the stabling area to cool Foxy out. Nothing, he decided, would ever top the rush of jumping a good cross-country course. Except maybe the thrill of standing on the dais at the Olympics and feeling a gold medal slipped over his neck . . .

"Parker? Parker? Hello. Are you all right?" Christina's voice pierced his dream, and he was back on the grassy road leading to the stabling area, his mud-caked field boots moving alongside Foxy's mud-covered bell boots.

"Hey," he said with a embarrassed grin.

"Hey, yourself," Christina said, walking up beside him. She was carrying a clean sweat sheet, which she placed over Foxy's steaming hindquarters. Breathless with excitement, she reached over to stroke Foxy's nose. "You were awesome as always, Foxy," she whispered.

"Wasn't she?" Parker exclaimed. He took off his helmet and ran his hand through his sweat-soaked dark hair. "She just soared over everything. I couldn't believe the way she took the trakehner. Like it was nothing."

"I'm sorry I missed it," Christina said. "Sam and I were standing by that crazy cabana fence. Sam said it was the toughest fence on the course, and Foxy didn't even blink."

When they reached the stabling area, Parker continued cooling Foxy, walking her slowly up and down in front of the stalls. Finally, when the mare was cool and breathing evenly, Christina helped Parker bathe her with warm water, removing every last trace of mud and sweat. Then they rubbed her down and put her back in her stall.

After Parker fastened the surcingles on Foxy's fly sheet, he stroked her velvety muzzle and gave her another Polo. "You were a star today. Get a good rest for stadium tomorrow," he said softly.

Then he stepped out of her stall and closed it.

Christina glanced at her watch. "If we hurry, we can catch another go or two. You can see what you're up against."

Parker sighed dramatically. "I'm already incredibly aware of who I'm riding against. I could hardly go anywhere this morning without seeing riders signing autographs."

Christina slipped her arm through his. "You're not half bad yourself, you know. And there's no one else here I'd rather go to the back-to-school dance with."

Parker grinned. Even though he'd been caught up

in the excitement of preparing for this trial, he hadn't forgotten that Henry Clay High's back-to-school dance was coming up. Christina was starting her senior year, and Parker was going to take her to his alma mater's big event.

"That's good to know. And how about tonight's exhibitors' party?"

"I think I could manage to be seen with you." Christina giggled.

"Do you think anyone would mind if I wore this?" Parker joked, glancing down at his muddy cross-country clothes.

Christina cocked her head. "You think anyone would notice if I came in my braiding overalls?"

Parker laughed. "On you, they look great."

A few minutes later they had stationed themselves by Catherine's Cabana, the fence Parker had jumped only a short while ago. It looked even more daunting from the ground. They watched a man on a huge chestnut take it much too fast. At the last minute the horse added a stride to save himself, and the rider was thrown over on his neck. Parker had to hand it to the horse—he narrowly missed disaster.

"Yikes," Christina murmured. "That wasn't pretty."

"You can say that again," said Parker, watching the team try to regain its composure and continue on. Soon they were up the hill and out of sight..

"Oh, look," Christina said, pointing down the path at the next rider, who was fast approaching. "What a funny-looking horse."

Parker turned his head to see Lyssa galloping toward them on Soldier Blue. They were coming along strong. *Too strong,* Parker thought as they drew closer. The gray horse's knees came close to knocking his chin, and his nostrils were flared. He snorted. "Well, at least she had the sense to put some tack on Old Big Foot—finally."

Christina shot him a puzzled look.

"Never mind." Parker's focus now shifted to Lyssa's approach to the drop fence. Once again he couldn't see her giving her horse a single aid. Sure, her horse was now wearing a saddle and bridle, but Lyssa rode no differently in the saddle than she had out of it. She was perfectly balanced, her hands light on the reins. At just the right distance away Blue made an adjustment, throwing his weight to his hindquarters, and sailed easily over the jump and galloped furiously on.

The crowd clapped wildly.

"Unbelievable," someone next to Parker said.

"Awesome," someone whispered from behind him.

Christina let out a low whistle. "Wow."

Parker shrugged. What was everyone making such

a big deal about? "It was just one fence," he muttered.

"True," Christina admitted. "But it wasn't easy, and that girl made it look like a little crossrail. What were you saying about her?"

Parker explained how he'd seen her in the schooling area riding bareback and bridleless. Christina raised her eyebrows, obviously impressed. Then she turned to watch the next rider. But Parker was distracted.

*All right, so she managed to get over a difficult jump. So did most of the other riders here. And they did it without showing off and schooling without tack. And without any gimmicks like wires around their horses' necks.*

After the last rider had ridden the course, Parker and Christina walked toward the boards, where the penalties and standings would be posted.

"It's getting chilly," Christina said suddenly, hugging herself. "And it looks like it's going to rain again."

Parker hadn't noticed it was cold, but they stopped at a concession stand for a cup of hot cocoa. While Christina waited in line, Parker tried to squeeze through the crowd so he could check on his standing.

"Hey, Townsend," called Oliver Flores, who was pushing his way back from the boards. "Way to go. You're in second place."

*But who's in first?* Parker's competitive side demanded silently.

As if reading his mind, Oliver added, "Some unknown from nowhere on a horse that looks like a mule is in first. Lyssa Hynde or Hyde or something. You ever heard of her?"

Parker shook his head.

"So that's her name," Christina said, coming up behind him. "This morning I overheard this lady in the stands talking about this amazing girl on an ugly horse who had a super dressage test. She's the one you saw riding without tack."

"I don't see how," Parker grumbled. "Dressage is all about how the horse and rider look together, whether they make a pleasing package." Remembering Lyssa's giant silver buckle, he added, "Those two look like something out of a spaghetti western."

Christina laughed. "Oh, come on. Look at how she handled that cabana fence compared to some of the rest of the riders. She was pretty incredible."

"Luck. Anyway, it's not over yet. Let's see how she is over the stadium-jumping course."

Christina arched her eyebrows. "Worried about your competition, Townsend?" she teased.

"Hardly. Foxy and I are going to give them a run for their money."

"Are you really as confident as you sound?"

Parker pulled Christina close to him and kissed her on the cheek. "Definitely," he assured her.

Parker left Christina and pushed through the crowd to the stewards' tent. He wanted to check the scorecards: his and Lyssa's. He couldn't believe Lyssa and her flea-bitten gray were actually beating him, not when he and Foxy had done their best. There was something about that girl he definitely did *not* like.

## 3

"YOU'RE NOT WEARING YOUR OVERALLS," PARKER WAILED with mock disappointment when he arrived that evening at Whitebrook to take Christina to the exhibitors' party.

"Sorry to let you down," Christina replied as she swept down the stairs. She was wearing a dark green sweater set and a black velvet skirt. Her strawberry blond hair was pulled back with glittering rhinestone clips that sparkled in the light.

"I can't say I'm that disappointed," Parker said. He lapsed into his English gentleman act and bowed low before taking Christina's hand and kissing it with a flourish. "You look absolutely stunning, dahling."

Christina giggled. "Well, you look rathah handsome yourself." She leaned over to straighten the lapel of Parker's dark blue jacket.

Christina's mom and dad, Ashleigh and Mike, appeared in the doorway. "Have a good time, you two," Ashleigh said, giving them each a big hug.

Parker could see that Christina was waiting for her dad to make his usual joke about coming and chaperoning the party, but he merely shook Parker's hand and clapped him on the back.

"Hey, have fun, you guys." Melanie yawned sleepily, shuffling up behind Ashleigh and Mike. Her short blond hair stuck up everywhere, and she was wearing gray sweats. "Chris said you rocked today, Parker. Way to go."

"Thanks," Parker replied. "What are you up to tonight?"

Melanie grinned and jerked her thumb toward the television behind her. "Hot date with the TV. I exercised, like, a million horses today, though, so I'm not up for much." Like Christina, Melanie was an apprentice jockey.

"Are Mel and Kevin still acting weird around each other?" Parker whispered to Christina after they'd slipped out the door. His best friend, Kevin McLean, and Melanie had been dating for the past few months but had recently broken up. Kevin's father, Ian McLean, was Whitebrook's head trainer. Since Melanie and Kevin both lived at Whitebrook, it had made for some awkward moments.

"Oh, they're all right, but it's definitely over between them," Christina answered. "At least for now."

They climbed into Parker's pickup truck.

"Dad didn't make his chaperon crack," Christina observed, smoothing her skirt.

Parker put the truck into gear and started down Whitebrook's long, winding drive. "Maybe he sees you're growing up," he said. "If only *my* parents saw the same thing."

Christina turned to him, her eyes full of sympathy. "Did they give you a hard time tonight?"

Parker nodded, but he didn't tell Christina about how they'd pounced on him earlier in the evening when he'd gone home to shower and change his clothes, demanding that he not go to what Lavinia called "that tacky exhibitors' party." He'd slipped up to his room, then darted out the servants' entrance and sneaked away like a thief. Parker didn't want to dwell on it any more by complaining about it to Christina.

Instead he told Christina a funny story about his English cousin who'd hijacked a pony from his uncle's racing stable and hid it in the garage of his fancy boarding school's stiff-lipped headmaster. The pony made quite a mess. Christina laughed until tears ran down her face.

"I guess your cousin is going to follow the family

tradition of getting thrown out of boarding school," she said wiping her eyes. "He'll grow out of it, though," she added, smiling up at Parker.

By the time they arrived at Thorndale's elegant clubhouse, Parker had cheered himself up and completely forgotten about his parents.

Tiny lights wrapped around the columns in the clubhouse entrance twinkled in the night, beckoning the party goers inside. Shiny brass chandeliers lighted up the large, elegant foyer and the ballroom beyond.

As Parker and Christina made their way to the punch table, they were surrounded by well-wishers and fellow riders eager to recap the exciting events of the day.

"That course sure pushed our limits," observed Cammie Dillon, whose horse, Dynamo, had fallen on his knees in the water jump but came through unhurt.

"Parker, you were one of the few riders who managed to avoid disaster at Catherine's Cabana," said Gillian Montgomery ruefully. She rubbed a sore shoulder. "Well, at least the EMTs who helped me up were cute. What was your secret, anyway?"

"No secret. It's all my horse," he said, ladling up some punch for Christina and himself. "She's brilliant."

"He talks about that horse like she's a superhero," Dave joked, turning to Gillian.

"Why not?" Parker shot back. "Foxy knows her way around a course."

"Well, maybe I should stable Mo near Foxy so she can give him some tips," Cammie replied, laughing.

"Excuse me a moment, everybody," Christina said, looking across the crowded room. "I see some classmates I want to say hi to. I'll be right back."

While Parker waited for Christina, he sipped his punch and looked around. A few couples were dancing off in the ballroom, but most of the exhibitors and their friends were standing and talking in small groups in the foyer. Most of the women were dressed up in dresses or skirts, like Christina. But his gaze fell on a girl talking to one of the show's officials. Unlike the others, she was wearing turquoise suede pants paired with a fringed suede vest of the same garish color. A giant silver buckle glinted at her waist. It was Lyssa, the wonder girl.

Just then Christina returned with her best friend, Katie Garrity, in tow. "Look who's here, Parker. Katie's aunt's one of the technical delegates."

"Hey, Katie. Do you think next time you could tell your aunt to schedule the rain for *after* my test?" Parker joked.

Katie smiled. "I'll be sure to do that."

They talked about the trial some more, and then the conversation switched to senior events at Henry Clay.

Parker found his attention wandering, and his gaze turned back to Lyssa. She stood out in the elegantly dressed crowd like a sore thumb. He even noticed a few people giving Lyssa's clothes a double take.

*Well, no wonder*, he thought. He was no snob, but there was no doubt that Lyssa was drawing attention to herself. She, however, didn't appear to be the least uncomfortable. She laughed and talked with people, and when the dancing started, Parker watched as she grabbed the weather-beaten man Parker had seen her with earlier that day and danced an energetic swing. When they finished, the crowd applauded.

*Showing off again*, Parker thought. Not to be out-done, he grabbed Christina, and they headed out on the dance floor. Parker didn't know how to dance the swing, but he had rhythm, and he and Christina made a lively pair. But Christina was more intent on watching the tackily dressed cowgirl and her partner.

"She's wild. Let's go introduce ourselves," Christina urged when the song ended. "I really want to meet her."

Parker smiled halfheartedly. He really didn't see why Christina found Lyssa so fascinating. "You go on over. I'm going to go say hi to Oliver. I heard he wants to buy a young horse to bring along, and I think Tor might have a prospect he'd be interested in."

Christina made her way through the crowd, and

Parker found Oliver, filling him in on the particulars of a promising gelding that Tor had just bought.

When Christina returned, her eyes were sparkling. "You should go talk to that girl, Parker. She really is the most interesting person I've ever met," she said, speaking up over the music, which had gotten louder as the evening wore on.

Interesting *is the word, all right*, Parker thought, watching Lyssa return to the dance floor with Dave. Dave was no swing expert, but Lyssa soon had him dipping and swirling while other dancers moved out of the way to avoid being kicked by Lyssa's cowboy boots.

Christina tilted her head. "Okay, so she takes some getting used to, but she's fun. Did you know that that buckle of hers is a trophy? It's got real sapphires and rubies in it. She's seventeen, and she's already been a rodeo queen and a barrel-racing champion."

"Barrel racing?"

Nodding, Christina continued. "She ropes cattle, too. She started to explain some of her training techniques, but it was hard to hear what she was saying over the music. She asked about the trainers around here, and I told her all about Sam. I could have talked to her all night."

Parker squeezed her hand. "I'm glad you didn't. I kind of hoped to dance with you again," he joked.

Christina pretended to punch him on the shoulder. "Are you ever serious?"

"Nope, never," Parker said. "C'mon, let's dance."

The next morning Parker arrived at the show grounds early. After mucking out Foxy's stall and feeding her, he changed into his riding clothes and covered them with old gray sweats while he groomed her and got ready. When he was finished, he shed his sweats and put on his black hunt coat.

Soon he had mounted up and was making his way over to the warm-up area.

"Here we go again," he muttered to Foxy after popping her over a few fences. He trotted Foxy out of the warm-up ring, keeping her on the bit, then loosened the reins and walked her over to the stadium-jumping ring.

At the far side Parker could see the dark green canopy covering the judges' stand and the three judges who studied each round with eagle eyes. He watched the riders go before him, each one taking rails down or refusing at the wall. Not one clean round. Parker realized that although the post-and-rail fences were big—some of the oxers were four-foot-six—they looked flimsy compared to the solid obstacles the competitors had jumped in cross-country the day before. But

Parker knew the fences were more complicated than they looked.

"Never underestimate stadium jumps," Sam had warned him time and time again. "They might look like nothing, but a good course designer will throw in a few surprises. Go to sleep for an instant, and you'll find yourself racking up faults."

"No faults today," Parker said aloud. He steered Foxy over to the gate, getting her attention by trotting figure eights until the announcer's voice told him he was on deck.

With that, Parker and Foxy entered the ring, picked up an even canter, and circled before their first combination. Foxy was on today; Parker could feel it right away. She jumped the first fence eagerly, her ears forward. But as they rounded the corner she fell in slightly, which threw off her stride just before the combination. Somehow she managed to clear it, but she rubbed the top pole on the second fence, and it came down. The crowd groaned. *Four faults*, Parker thought, but he collected himself and headed toward the fake stone wall with determination, the most intimidating fence on the course. Always up for a challenge, Foxy sailed over it in stride and cantered on to the next line, a tricky diagonal triple. Parker rated her just before she jumped in, and she landed perfectly. One stride, jump, jump. Perfect. Foxy changed leads as they rounded the corner, and Parker kept his leg on for the final line—the wishing wells, then six long strides to a narrow vertical. Six, five, four, three, two, one. Foxy took off over the last jump, her hooves throwing up grass clods. They landed clear, and Parker grinned and stroked Foxy's neck as they flew past the timer.

"Never mind those faults, girl," Parker said as they rode out of the ring. "We can still win this one. There's no way that cowgirl can do better than that."

Parker dismounted and walked Foxy up and down to cool her. Then he stood by the out gate, watching as Lyssa and Blue cantered into the ring, circling easily, almost lazily, and making their way toward the first line. Blue looked like he was asleep, and Parker was certain he'd take down a pole. The crowd gasped as Blue lifted his big knees at the last minute and cleared the first combination and then the second as if they were made of toothpicks. Lyssa was smiling and looked as relaxed as if she were on a trail ride, and she and Blue rounded the corner as if they had all the time in the world.

"You'd think she could wake up that horse," Parker mumbled to himself, drawing in his breath as Blue took off from an impossibly close distance at the wall. It was as if he jumped straight *up*.

"That horse is so athletic," whispered a girl on a chestnut who halted next to Parker.

*That rider is so passive,* Parker thought, although he really did admire the way Lyssa let her horse do his job without interference. Only before the bounce did Lyssa give Blue a bit of leg, and Blue responded by lengthening his massive stride slightly and jumping with precision. From then on, Lyssa left him alone, and Blue seemed comfortable jumping whatever came his way.

*Lyssa's going to go clear,* Parker thought with dismay as the team headed toward the last line. Sure enough, Blue's floppy ears flicked back and forth as he thundered out the last six strides and approached the narrow vertical squarely. Then he soared over it, throwing a triumphant buck when he landed. Lyssa leaned forward to hug the big gray around the neck as the announcer's voice crackled over the loudspeaker.

"A clear round for Lyssa Hynde on Soldier Blue!"

Disappointment sat heavy in Parker's stomach as the crowd exploded in thunderous applause.

The tacky, show-off cowgirl had won the trial. She'd beaten him. Parker rode in to receive his red ribbon, still not believing what had happened.

"Congratulations," he forced himself to say as Lyssa rode past, happily clutching her silver cup, the blue ribbon flapping from Blue's bridle.

Placing second at the advanced level at a horse trial like Thorndale was very impressive, Parker reminded himself as he drove home from Thorndale that afternoon. But he'd have to make sure he and Foxy *won* the next competition, especially if Lyssa and Blue were there.

"One horse trial down, one big three-day to go," Parker said aloud as he turned up his CD player. "Then Olympics, here we come—I hope." He glanced at the red ribbon he'd set on the seat next to him, then looked in the side mirrors on his truck to double-check the horse trailer rolling along behind. He could just see the side of Foxy's head through the small window in the front of the trailer. She was going home to a warm bran mash and a few days of well-deserved rest.

As Parker drove toward Whisperwood he found himself wishing Christina had been able to see the stadium jumping. Now that she was so busy at the track and exercising horses at Whitebrook, opportunities to be together were few and far between. The exhibitors' party had been a rare exception.

Turning into Whisperwood's wide drive, Parker drove under the decorated wood sign:

WHISPERWOOD FARM

TOR AND SAMANTHA NELSON

"We're here, girl," Parker called through the window.

Foxy neighed appreciatively, and several of her

41

stablemates whinnied back. Parker unloaded her, pulled off her shipping boots, and led her toward the whitewashed barn with its high beamed ceilings and huge hayloft. The mare pulled impatiently at her lead, plainly glad to be home.

Several of Sam's students rushed up and crowded around them, demanding to see his ribbon and hear all about the trial.

"I hope I get good enough to ride at Thorndale one day," said Kaitlin Boyce enviously. She was leasing Sterling Dream from Sam, who'd bought the dapple gray mare from Christina. It hadn't been an easy decision for Christina to sell Sterling, but when she'd turned her attention from eventing to racing, she found she no longer had time to keep a talented horse like Sterling in top form. Parker knew Christina was thrilled at how well Kaitlin got along with Sterling.

Parker patted the girl's shoulder. "You will. You and Sterling are on your way."

After Parker had unloaded his trailer, he mixed up the bran mash and headed toward the feed room, where the vitamin supplements were kept. Just then he heard the loud pop of an engine backfiring and a beat-up, dusty white truck rattled into the drive. The trailer it was pulling was equally ugly and equally beat-up, with a purple mountain scene hand-painted on one side. Blue smoke poured out the exhaust pipe as the truck groaned to a stop in front of the barn. Even from a distance Parker could read the large bumper sticker: TO RIDE OR NOT TO RIDE? WHAT A STUPID QUESTION!

"That thing come here to die?" asked Jodi, one of Whisperwood's grooms, who was walking by carrying a bucket of soapy water left over from a tack-cleaning session.

Parker snorted and watched curiously as the driver of the truck hopped out and lowered the ramp on the trailer. Maybe Samantha had rescued another diamond in the rough from an auction—some poor, scrawny horse that would one day become a champion. She'd done that more than once in the past.

It wasn't until Parker got closer that he saw who the driver was—Lyssa Hynde!

"Now, what is *she* doing here?" Parker mumbled in amazement. He'd been hoping that after the trial was over, she'd go back to her cow pasture or circus or wherever she came from and he'd never have to see her again.

A moment later Sam pulled into the drive in the Nelsons' dark blue rig and climbed out to help Lyssa unload Blue. The two led the horse toward the barn to a chorus of shrill whinnies of greeting from the other horses, who watched from their stalls.

*Probably can't believe their eyes*, Parker thought, shaking his head at the sight of the unattractive gray horse with his floppy ears and oversized hooves.

As they drew closer Sam waved.

"Hey, Parker," she called. "Would you grab a tube of Corona out of the medicine chest? Blue got a nick on his hock somehow. I'd like to put a dab on it."

"Uh, sure," Parker said. He was glad to have something to do other than stare at Lyssa and her sorry excuse for a horse.

*Beauty is as beauty does.* Parker smiled as he recalled something his grandfather, a respected horseman, was always saying. If Clay were here right now instead of fishing with old friends in Ireland, that was probably exactly what he'd tell Parker.

After locating the bright yellow tube of antiseptic cream, Parker turned around and almost bumped into Christina, who'd just come through the tack-room door.

"Hey, what are you doing here?" he asked, surprised.

"Hi," she said breathlessly. "I need some scissors and gauze. Sam wants to wrap Blue's cut. I came over from Whitebrook the minute Sam called. Isn't this exciting?"

"Isn't what exciting?" Parker asked, feeling confused. He rummaged around for the scissors and package of gauze. Then they headed up the barn aisle where Sam was waiting.

"Lyssa's staying here at Whisperwood," Christina explained, sounding surprised that Parker hadn't already heard.

Parker frowned. "What do you mean, staying here?"

"She's boarding Blue here until the Deer Springs three day. Sam's going to help her since her trainer has to go back home, and Lyssa's going to work for Sam in exchange."

Parker gaped at her, amazed. Then he cleared his throat. *Make a joke*, he told himself. "But there aren't any cows for her to rope. And I don't think Tor will like it if she tries to rope his dogs." It came out sounding meaner than he'd wanted it to.

Christina shot him a look. "Ha ha."

Parker paused. "Why can't she just go *home* until Deer Springs?"

"Parker, how do you think she's going to get that horse home to Montana and back again and still have him fit and ready for a big four-star event like Deer Springs?"

"She's from Montana?"

Christina gave him an amused grin. "I thought you always studied your competition—you should know what size shoe her horse wears by now. I mean, after all, she beat you at the trial and all."

"As if I didn't notice," Parker said in a sarcastic

tone. He didn't need Christina to rub in the fact that he had come in second to Lyssa.

"I'm sorry. But second place isn't too bad, you know," she reminded him.

"Hey, I'm happy with it. But why did she have to come here? She could have stayed somewhere else."

"Do you know a better eventing trainer than Sam around here, Parker?" Christina said, raising her eyebrows at him.

At that, Parker threw up his hands. "No, you're right."

When they got to the crossties, he handed the tube of cream silently to Sam, who turned to tend to Soldier Blue's hock. Parker and Christina drew back to give Sam room. Lyssa stood at Blue's head, a look of concern on her face.

"I've got to warn you, Blue's a big baby when it comes to being hurt," Lyssa said.

"Most horses are," Parker replied.

"But Blue's a megababy," Lyssa countered.

"Nothing Sam hasn't seen before." Parker locked eyes with Lyssa. He wasn't sure why he was baiting her, but she seemed unfazed. She didn't turn away.

Just as Sam swabbed the area with some warm water, Blue coiled up and leaped away, snorting and lashing out with his enormous hoof. Sam scooted back to avoid being kicked.

"He's sure strong," Sam commented.

"Aww, he's just a big teddy bear," Lyssa crooned.

*Some teddy bear*, Parker thought. From where he stood, he figured Blue must be at least seventeen-and-a-half hands tall.

"Yikes, that must really sting," Christina said, peering more closely at the wound when Blue stopped dancing around. "How did he do it?"

Lyssa looked lovingly at her horse. "Blue hates being trailered, so he usually kicks up a ruckus."

"Do you want me to get a chain to run over his nose so you can hold him?" Parker asked.

"No thanks, I think I can get him to stand a little quieter," Lyssa replied.

"I'll get the chain," said Parker, but Lyssa clamped her hand on his arm. Parker was surprised at how strong she was.

"I'll handle it," she said with a slight edge to her voice.

When she released Parker's arm, she stood on the toes of her cowboy boots and took Blue's big, floppy ears in her hands. Then she murmured something into his left ear. Within seconds Blue lowered his head, his eyes half closed and his lower lip hanging.

"Okay, try again," Lyssa said in a low, singsong tone.

Sam approached the cut gingerly, but this time the

horse stood quietly as she applied the thick cream to his hock.

"How did you get him to do that?" Sam asked, her eyes wide when she'd finished.

Lyssa's eyes didn't leave her horse. "Get him to do what?"

Parker glanced at Christina, who mouthed, "Wow!"

"Get him to change gears so quickly," Sam said. She reached for the gauze and scissors and began to wrapped the sore area.

Lyssa let go of Blue's ears, but he remained perfectly still until Sam was completely finished. "Oh," she answered finally. "Once he knew what I wanted, it was no big deal."

*What a show-off.* Parker rolled his eyes, then walked off to get Foxy's vitamin supplements.

A moment later Christina joined him outside Foxy's stall.

"That was pretty cool," Christina said in a low voice.

"Humph," Parker said absently, watching Foxy bury her nose in her mash and supplements. He closed the stall door and latched it securely. "Listen, do you have time to grab a quick bite? I haven't eaten since this morning, and I'm starved."

Christina nodded. "Me too I have a huge essay due

for English tomorrow, and I haven't even started on it."

"Aw, you'll get it done. You always do. Anyway, we haven't had much time to be alone together. How does Joey's sound?" Parker asked, knowing Christina could never resist a plate of the diner's fries.

"Greasy, but good," replied Christina.

"I have to unhitch my trailer first," Parker said.

"Okay. Let me run and see if Sam and Lyssa need any more help. I'll meet you out front in fifteen minutes."

Parker put away the rest of his things in the tack room and then washed the barn grit off his hands as best he could. When he walked outside, Christina was already climbing into the passenger side of his truck. Parker strode up and opened the driver's side door. Just then Lyssa walked by, carrying a load of tack from her rig.

Parker started the engine, furrowing his brow. "A western saddle? Whoa. Check out the conchos. Do you think that's all real silver?"

"Probably," Christina said impatiently. "Lyssa said her uncle Cal had to fly back to Montana this morning. Do you think she'll be lonely hanging around here tonight?"

"I doubt it. I'm sure she brought her mechanical bull with her. Maybe she'll set it up and teach the grooms how to ride it. Or maybe she can teach them how to swing dance," Parker cracked.

"Very funny, Townsend," Christina retorted as she rolled down her window. "Hey, Lyssa! Want to come for a burger at Joey's?" she called.

Parker felt a flash of irritation. Normally his theory was the more the merrier. But Lyssa wasn't exactly his idea of merry. *Weird* was more like it. And *annoying*.

"I want to make sure Blue settles in," Lyssa replied. "Maybe some other time."

Parker barely hid his relief. "Why'd you do that?" he asked Christina when they had driven safely out of earshot.

Christina pushed a strand of hair out of her face. "Why not?" she asked, sounding defensive. "I wanted to talk to her. I keep hearing all these mysterious rumors about her, and I need to find out if they're true. Besides, I like her."

"What rumors?" Parker demanded.

"Well, someone said that she's home schooled."

Parker didn't comment. *So?* he thought. *Big deal*.

"She has her own Web site," Christina added.

"So do lots of people."

"Also, when I was coming out of the ladies' room at the party last night, I heard someone say Blue was once struck by lightning."

"I can believe that," Parker said, putting his truck

50

into gear. "Maybe that's why he's so ugly." He began to laugh but stopped when he saw the look on Christina's face.

Christina scowled. "That wasn't the nicest thing you've ever said."

Instantly Parker was sorry for his nasty comment. "I guess he doesn't have to be pretty to jump the way he does."

"You're just spoiled because Foxy is both beautiful and talented," Christina teased.

"Yeah, I guess I am. You should have seen her today. She was such a pro."

"I wish I could have seen it," Christina said. "But I've got so much work to do to get Star ready for the Derby, sometimes I wonder if I can really do it all."

"You will," Parker said loyally. He leaned over and gave her hand a reassuring squeeze.

Christina smiled. "Star has been going great. We decided to enter him in the Bluegrass Stakes. I'm nervous about it, but Mom thinks he's definitely ready."

"Don't worry, Chris. Ashleigh wouldn't push you if you weren't ready," Parker assured her.

Once they had sat down in their favorite booth at Joey's, Christina brought up Lyssa again, to Parker's dismay.

"I don't care if you think she's weird. I'm really glad she's staying at Whisperwood," she said, taking a giant bite of her gooey cheeseburger.

Parker toyed with his straw. "I still don't see why. So what if she won today? She got lucky."

Christina shrugged. "Maybe. But I still think there's something unique about her. I can't tell you what it is, but she knows horses."

"We know lots of people who know horses. In fact, we hardly know anyone who doesn't."

"Yeah, but, it's different with her. I mean, did you see the way she got Blue to calm down so quickly just by holding his ears and talking to him?"

Parker flashed Christina an amused grin. "Aha, so you think she's one of those horse whisperers who can tame a wild horse by mumbling the right words into his ear?"

Christina met his gaze but didn't say anything.

"No way. Tell me you don't believe in that voodoo."

"All I know is Lyssa's got a way with horses, and I want to learn what I can from her," Christina insisted.

"She can't teach you anything. She's into shortcuts and gimmicks. Don't let her fool you."

Pushing back her hair, Christina smiled at Parker. "I know you don't believe a word you're saying. You saw for yourself that she can ride. It takes more than luck to win an event against that kind of competition!"

Parker shrugged resignedly. "How about we agree to disagree?"

## 4

*BEEP, BEEP, BEEP.* IT WAS STILL DARK WHEN PARKER'S ALARM went off on Monday morning. He rolled over to see that the lighted dial read 5:45 A.M. There was no point in getting up, he decided, switching it off. After the rigors of the horse trial Foxy needed the day off. He'd probably just hand-walk her lightly after his morning classes. He was about to doze off when he glanced lazily at the pile of textbooks stacked on his desk. He might as well get to campus early and use the time to put in some extra study hours—he didn't want to get behind in his first year of college. He could check on Foxy on his way over to the university. Sitting up, Parker pushed back his fluffy duvet and climbed out of bed.

After a quick shower, he dressed in jeans and sneakers, hoping he wouldn't waken the servants. One of his parents' maids, Connie, had a grandmotherly fondness for him and was always slipping him cookies or treats to give to Foxy. She meant well, but if she heard him rustling about, she'd get up right away and start fussing over him, insisting on making him a huge breakfast.

Parker crept quietly down the back stairs, but as he stepped into the vast kitchen he saw that it was already too late. His father was talking on the phone at the head of the table, surrounded by serving platters heaped high with French toast and eggs Benedict. Parker heard Brad say goodbye to someone in Japanese and hang up. Motioning impatiently to Connie that he wanted more coffee, Brad glanced at Parker and loaded up his plate. Just the sight of the rich food made Parker's stomach turn. He never understood how anyone could eat like that so early in the morning.

"Good morning," Parker greeted his father with forced politeness.

Brad Townsend's eyes slid over his son, narrowing as he took in Parker's worn jeans and unlaced sneakers. "You're up early," he said coolly.

*I'm usually up this early. It's just that you never notice,* Parker wanted to say. Instead he simply nodded and eased toward the back door.

"I've got some work to do at school," he muttered. It wasn't a total lie. After all, he *was* going to the library right after he checked on his horse.

"Mmmm," Brad said, looking him up and down. "That the way you college boys dress for class these days? My professors would never have stood for that."

Parker groaned inwardly, hoping his dad would save him the lecture about his Ivy League college days. He couldn't wait to get out of there. Parker's dad held up the sports section of the newspaper, which featured a photo of Lyssa and Soldier Blue soaring over the huge brush fence at Thorndale. BLUE TAKES THE BLUE, screamed the headline.

"Second place, huh?" Brad asked with an unmistakable sneer. "Here you are wasting your time in a second-rate sport, and you can't even beat out a country bumpkin riding a flea-bitten nag. I ought to tell my father to buy you a real horse next time."

Parker's blood pounded in his ears. How dare his father insult Foxy? He swallowed hard and managed to bite back a nasty retort. "Whatever," he said neutrally, trying not to let his dad see how much the remark hurt.

Brad Townsend's face reddened, and he looked like he was about to make another attack. Luckily the phone rang just then, and Parker waited to bolt out the door until his dad picked it up and started shouting into the receiver.

Moments later Parker was on the road, munching a doughnut and sipping from a paper cup of strong coffee. It was way better than any fancy food eaten in the company of his disapproving father.

The sun was just rising as Parker pulled into the parking area at Whisperwood. Loud whinnies pierced the air, and hungry horses rattled their feed bins, waiting for the grooms to fill them with feed. Parker took in a deep lungful of cool morning air as he walked to Foxy's stall. She was still half asleep, standing with her head low in a deep bed of straw.

"Good morning, sleepyhead," Parker crooned. "Did you have a good snooze?"

He ducked into the stall and checked Foxy's legs to make sure they hadn't stocked up during the night. Sometimes a horse's legs swelled from standing in its stall after a hard workout. But Foxy's legs were tight—she looked fine. Parker adjusted her sheet and stepped out of her stall, latching the door securely.

He reached out and scratched Foxy's muzzle. "I'll see ya after Business 101. Then we'll go for a nice, long walk. You take it easy today. You deserve it."

It was hard for Parker to pay attention to his droning professor that morning. Sitting way in the back of the huge lecture hall, he kept replaying all three phases of the Thorndale trial. His sticky canter transition in dressage. His exhilarating cross-country ride. Closing his eyes, he could feel Foxy's firepower underneath him as she charged through the water jump. Then his mind leaped to stadium jumping and their unfortunate rail. They had done well, but they had made mistakes. Would they do better at Deer Springs? He sincerely hoped so.

Finally class was over, and Parker was once again rumbling along in his truck on the way to Whisperwood. As he pulled into the drive he was surprised to see a couple of cars he didn't recognize in the parking area. Maybe Sam and Tor had some visitors this morning. New clients, perhaps. Parker was glad. The Nelsons deserved to make a huge success of their operation.

But as he neared the barn he saw Lyssa standing by the tack-room door, talking to two big-shouldered men in rumpled khakis. One was writing furiously in a little notebook. The other was holding a little tape recorder. The men weren't rich horse owners looking for a topflight eventing barn. Definitely not. Parker had seen the type before—they were reporters.

"Miss Hynde, how did it feel to beat out some of the best eventers in the country?" he heard one of the men ask.

Annoyance shot through him. The press had already swarmed Lyssa the second she finished her victory gallop yesterday. Wasn't her win old news by now?

Lyssa waved to Parker, then turned back to the

reporters. Parker couldn't hear her reply, but the men laughed at whatever it was and peppered her with more questions. When he walked past, he heard one of the reporters remark, "That's Parker Townsend; he took second."

*Second*, Parker thought as he strode down the barn aisle. Hearing the reporter say it in that dismissive tone made it sound like a bad word. Maybe his father was right—he would never be more than second-rate.

A knot had formed in Parker's stomach. *Don't think like that*, he scolded himself as he buckled Foxy's leather halter. His grandfather had always warned him against listening to his doubts. "Never take counsel of your fears," he was fond of saying.

For a moment Parker leaned against Foxglove and drank in the sweet smell of shampoo, hay, and horse, drawing strength from her presence. He rubbed her halter's brass nameplate with his sleeve and led her out of her stall and down the barn aisle.

Once Foxy was on crossties, Parker lost himself in the comforting routine of grooming. After he picked out Foxy's hooves, he took a firm-bristled brush and went through the loose hairs from her coat. Then he finger combed her crinkly mane and glossy, thick tail. His grandfather had taught him long ago to use only his fingers to separate the tangles. "That's the secret to a beautiful, full tail," he'd said.

Parker ran a soft body-brush over Foxy's sleek hindquarters and wiped her face with a cloth, touching up her freshly clipped muzzle with a dab of baby oil to keep it soft.

"C'mon, girl, you're beautiful. Now let's go for a walk," Parker said, unclipping the ties and leading her down the aisle.

He glared at the reporters still surrounding Lyssa by the tack-room door. "A *long* walk," he added.

Foxy tossed her head as they passed the noisy group. Just then Parker heard Lyssa thank the reporters and tell them she didn't have time for any more questions.

"Daylight's turning to darkness," she said with an exaggerated drawl Parker hadn't heard her use before. "I can't stand around here jawing anymore. Hey, Parker, wait up."

Parker turned around to see Lyssa loping up behind him. "I've got to walk Blue, too. Mind if I join you? I don't know my way around here too well."

"Uh, sure," Parker muttered. How could he say that her company was the last thing he wanted?

Foxy waited impatiently, her silky black tail swishing at imaginary deerflies, while Lyssa got Soldier Blue out of his stall. As she approached, Parker glanced at the words silk-screened on her bright orange T-shirt. SHUT UP AND RIDE! Lyssa's shiny dark hair was braided in pigtails and tied off with turquoise leather thongs.

*Going for the Native American princess look,* Parker scoffed silently. His attention shifted as he saw that Blue was lumbering several yards behind Lyssa.

"Uh—I think you forgot his halter," Parker said.

Lyssa shook her head. "Naw," she said. "Blue doesn't like halters."

Parker gave Foxy a gentle tug on her well-oiled lead and started down one of the leafy paths that led toward Whisperwood's back pastures. "He doesn't like halters, he doesn't like trailers, he doesn't like bridles, he doesn't like saddles. What else doesn't your horse like?"

Lyssa laughed lightly. "I can see you don't approve. It wasn't my idea, though. Blue's told me what he wanted, and he was sure stubborn about it."

Parker regarded her for a moment, walking serenely alongside her horse, who didn't seem to notice that he could take off whenever he chose.

"Do you always listen to your horse?" he asked.

She looked serious. "Always," she said solemnly. "But that doesn't mean I let him get away with anything. We made a deal a long time ago. He was born on the range, and he didn't take to being gentled all that well. I gentled him, but I didn't want to break his spirit. I listen to him and let him be as free as possible. But when we're working, he listens to me. It's pretty simple."

Parker looked at the girl. "You don't really expect me to believe that nonsense."

"Believe it or don't believe it. It really doesn't matter to me."

With that, Lyssa pulled abruptly ahead of Parker, her cowboy boots crunching on the leaves. Knowing he'd been rude, he moved up beside her again. "I didn't mean it like that. It's just . . . different than our ways here, you know. I guess you find Kentucky pretty weird after what you're used to."

"Some. It's sure not like Montana. At all," Lyssa said.

"I can believe that. I've traveled a lot, but I've never been to Montana. What's it like?"

The girl's bright blue eyes grew soft. "What's there to say? It's beautiful; you can ride all day and not bump into anyone. There are mountain peaks with snow on them all year round. It's just . . . home, and I really don't like to be away."

Parker smiled and looked around at the familiar sight of white fences surrounding the paddocks and the golden canopy of trees overhead. "I know what you mean. I got sent away to this school in England for a while. I hated being away from home. Er . . . home being Kentucky, I mean."

"You didn't mind being away from your *parents*, though, eh?" Lyssa said, glancing at him sideways.

Parker shrugged, embarrassed at revealing himself to a stranger. "Yeah, something like that."

"I'm just the opposite. My parents own Black Thunder ranch near Billings. It used to be a cattle ranch only, but then we turned it into a dude ranch. We have people from all over the world come to ride and learn to rope and things. I help my parents run the place."

"Sounds like a lot of work," Parker said.

"Oh, it is. But it's a lot of fun, too. You should see some of the people that show up. One time this woman wore stockings and high heel sandals to a roundup. She was actually planning to ride like that."

Soon Lyssa was entertaining Parker with stories of the city slickers who turned up at her ranch, including an overworked Chicago executive who'd tried to run his corporation from his horse via cell phone while driving cattle.

"This one guy kept trying to talk on his cell phone while riding. He got so mad every time he got disconnected—yelling and stampeding the cattle. Finally he tossed that phone over a canyon wall and decided to quit his job and became a cowboy poet!" Lyssa exclaimed.

Parker cracked a smile in spite of himself. He was used to being the storyteller, but he had to admit that Lyssa knew how to capture an audience.

"So tell me about Blue's training," Parker said casually while they walked along.

"Not much to tell. I fell in love with him," Lyssa said, lighting up. "But he sure was a mean colt, and my daddy talked about shooting him sometimes."

"Whoa."

"I was worried sick my dad was serious, so I started trying some Native American training methods I learned from my uncle," Lyssa went on. "It was slow, but eventually it started to work. Blue got really good at working cattle. Then I started barrel racing him. He was always jumping out of the pasture, so . . ." She paused, sighing. "I decided to try eventing, and here we are."

Parker knew there was more to the story. After all, a horse didn't go from being a cow horse to winning the advanced division of a big horse trial like Thorndale overnight. But he could tell Lyssa was tired of talking, and he didn't press her with any more questions. Parker enjoyed walking along in silence, stopping to let their horses graze now and then. He and Foxy weren't going to do much more relaxing between now and the critical three day coming up, that was for sure.

When they got back to the stable area, Parker heard Lyssa mutter a soft, "Oh, not again."

His gaze followed hers to a white van with the letters WKEN emblazoned on the sides in large, block letters that was just pulling into the stable area.

Two journalists jumped out of the van and walked purposefully toward them, one nearly crashing into a groom, who was carrying several buckets of feed supplements. "Miss Hynde, Miss Hynde, may we get some clips of you and that fabulous horse of yours for the evening news?"

"Look," said the cameraman. "He's not even wearing a leash!"

The other journalist moved forward eagerly. "Does your horse do any tricks?"

"Well, yes, he does. Let me check with Sam first to make sure we aren't disrupting anyone, but I guess we could show you a few things," Lyssa said, glancing at Parker.

Parker shrugged. *She's only pretending to be modest,* he thought contemptuously. *She's eating this up.* "Have fun," he said hollowly.

Just as Parker turned to lead Foxy away the cameraman switched on his camera. Foxy started at the loud whirring noise, and Parker glared at the cameraman's back while he tried to settle her down.

"Excuse me, could you move that wheelbarrow? I'd like to set up some lights here," he heard one of the journalists ask a groom.

Leading Foxy toward the crossties, Parker shook his head. This was unbelievable. Whisperwood was turning into Hollywood!

After picking out Foxy's feet, Parker put her away in her stall. He was just rearranging his grooming box when he heard Christina's voice. Spinning around, he saw her coming down the aisle, her reddish ponytail bouncing.

"Hey, this is becoming a regular thing," he said happily.

"Wow. Did you see all those reporters?" she asked.

Parker nodded. "Yeah. But when you and Star won the Laurel Stakes, there were even more."

Christina shrugged. "Hey, did you know Blue can turn a water faucet on and off by himself? They filmed him doing it and spraying one of the grooms with the hose."

"Oh," Parker answered unenthusiastically.

"And he can walk up stairs."

"They ought to charge admission," Parker joked bitterly. "Blue, the ugliest wonder horse in the world!"

Usually she laughed at his jokes, but Christina didn't smile.

"Hey, lighten up," he said weakly.

Christina shrugged. "She's just giving them what they want."

"Maybe. I'm surprised Sam doesn't mind, though."

"C'mon. All this attention is amazing for Sam and Tor's business. Think of the publicity they'll get."

"The wrong kind of publicity," Parker muttered.

Christina pursed her lips. "How can it be wrong? An unknown girl wins an huge horse trial against top eventing riders—and she decides to train with Sam. That's good publicity if you ask me. Besides, I was listening to what she told the reporters, and everything she said makes total sense. I'm going to see if she can give me some pointers with Star."

At that Parker let out his breath in a loud whoosh. "Star? You want to teach him how to turn on a hose?"

Silence.

"Come on, Chris. You're not falling for her nonsense, too, are you?"

"I don't happen to think it's nonsense. It's just different for a change. I think it's cool."

"And I think that girl has worked her horse whisperer voodoo on you."

Christina turned away, tossing her ponytail over her shoulder. "What's wrong—are you jealous?"

5

"I KNOW YOU'D RATHER BE JUMPING, BUT IF WE WANT TO impress the Olympic selection people, we've got to work on dressage," Parker murmured to Foxglove as he tacked her up on Friday after his classes at the university.

He sighed and climbed up on the blue mounting block. Over the last couple of days Parker had been concentrating on roadwork for conditioning, occasionally popping over some low fences. As usual, the thought of flatwork did not appeal to him today. A light wind was kicking up the colorful autumn leaves, and Foxy snorted and pranced as Parker settled into the saddle.

Clucking Foxy forward, he made his way to the dressage arena, where Sam was waiting on Sterling.

Kaitlin had twisted her ankle at school and couldn't ride, so Sam was schooling her.

"Afternoon, Parker," Sam called as he rode into the rectangular area. "Getting psyched up for Deer Springs?"

"You bet. I've started running again and working out to get ready for it. I ran four miles this morning."

Sam smiled. "Good for you. You think Foxy is ready to school, or is she still tired from the trial?"

"Oh, she's feeling good, all right," Parker said with a laugh. "I've already jumped her a little this week. And she's feeling full of herself today."

"Like her owner, huh?" Sam was always teasing Parker about his unfailing belief in himself.

Parker grinned and suddenly realized that it wasn't quite true anymore. Over the last few days he'd found himself wondering more and more if he'd been way too optimistic, thinking he'd be picked for the Olympics.

"Try getting her on the bit now. Move her up at the walk. Get her working from behind," Sam instructed, drowning out his thoughts.

Parker rolled his eyes. Serpentines and figure eights—how boring. But if he wanted to even dream about the Olympics, he was going to have to work. Hard.

He started Foxy at a working walk, bending her around his legs and asking her to move forward. Then he asked for a rising trot, collecting her a little and guiding her around a twenty-meter circle. Back on the rail, Foxy extended the trot, her hooves seeming to float above the ground. They went on to leg yields, shoulder-ins, half passes, and passages.

"Keep her frame. Support her with the outside rein. Eyes up," Sam instructed.

"Come on, girl," Parker muttered.

Something wasn't clicking today. Foxy was using every blowing leaf as an excuse to evade the bit, and Parker felt tense. He ordered himself to relax, afraid he'd telegraph his tension to Foxy, but it was no use.

"Work with her, Parker, not against her," Sam called from the center of the arena.

Parker frowned. He was working, but Foxy wasn't listening. Her back was hollow, her nose was in the air, and her hind end was simply trailing along for the ride.

Sam watched for a while, her hands resting on the pommel of Sterling's saddle.

"All right, let her walk," she said finally. "Why don't we try something I learned from Lyssa this morning? It's a Native American concept where the horse learns to follow the *itancan*, or leader."

"Huh?" Parker said. "You've got to be joking."

"No, I'm not," Sam insisted. "It's very interesting. Lyssa says—"

But Parker had already tuned her out. *Lyssa says—* he'd had enough of what Lyssa said, from *everyone*.

"Did you catch that, Parker?"

He shook his head irritably. "Sam, if you don't mind, I think I'll skip it for now."

Sam raised an eyebrow. "I know you don't think dressage is the most exciting thing in the world, but it's vital, and your jumping can only get better for it. Parker, you of all people know that."

Parker blew out an exasperated breath. "I do, I know. But I think we'll be better off tomorrow when we're both in a better frame of mind."

"You can't run from snags when you encounter them. You've got to work through them," Sam said softly. "And I think you'll really like this new technique Lyssa—"

Parker held up a hand, feeling terrible for doing so. He never contradicted Sam, but he couldn't stand it anymore. He had to get out of the ring, away from her critical glances and away from Lyssa's mumbo-jumbo horse sense.

"Maybe Foxy's burned out. I'm going take her for a little trail ride," he muttered defensively. "I don't want to force her." Swinging away from Sam and Sterling, Parker headed out for the opening in the low white rail of Whisperwood's dressage ring.

"With all due respect, Parker, I think you're making

a mistake," Sam said. "I'll see you here at three-thirty tomorrow," she ordered.

Parker nodded and turned toward the path that ran between Whisperwood's pastures. He couldn't believe what he'd just done. But he couldn't imagine plodding around in endless circles, listening to Lyssa's wacky theories coming out of Sam's mouth.

"It's not like we're not doing anything; we'll *condition*. We'll do some gallops, some intervals," Parker argued with himself. But as he said it he knew he was kidding himself. He and Foxy needed as much instruction as they could get before Deer Springs. Especially in dressage.

*Tomorrow,* Parker promised himself. *Tomorrow we'll sort out our trouble areas.* He lifted his chin and let the early September sun warm his face, determined to forget his worries and relax.

When Parker and Foxy returned to the barn, he was glad to see Christina walking through the stable yard. Her steady good spirits were just what he needed.

"Hi," he called as he dismounted and loosened Foxy's girth. "Wow. This is the second, no, third time you've come here this week. I'm honored."

Christina's hazel eyes sparkled. "I didn't think I'd have a chance, but I finished my barn chores early, so Melanie and I decided to drop by before we start our homework."

"Melanie's here?" Parker asked in surprise.

"Uh-huh," Christina answered vaguely. "So where were you? I thought you had dressage with Sam today."

"Foxy and I blew off our lesson," Parker said, pulling off his saddle and hooking Foxy on crossties.

Christina frowned. "Blew off your lesson? How come?"

Parker shrugged and began brushing Foxy rhythmically, humming while he did so. Christina looked like she wanted to ask more, and Parker was glad when she went off to see Sterling instead.

"Want to get a cup of coffee?" Parker asked when Christina walked by on the way back from Sterling's stall.

"Thanks," Christina said. "But I'm watching Lyssa ride. She's going to show me some exercises she does with Blue. Melanie was curious, too; that's why she's here."

*Lyssa—again*, Parker thought, but made no comment. He combed out Foxy's long, silky tail with his fingers and tried not to let his face register his annoyance.

"Well, how about tomorrow, then?" he suggested.

"Can't." Christina shook her head. "Mel and I are going to go to the mall to look for dresses for the back-to-school dance."

"Oh. Is Melanie going to the dance?" Parker asked casually. He didn't want to be nosy, but unless he'd missed something, she and Kevin still hadn't gotten back together.

Christina looked uncomfortable. "Yeah. She didn't really want to, but this guy in our English class named Jeff asked her. She turned him down at first, but I talked her into it. She's got to have fun, right?"

"I guess," Parker replied. He unhooked Foxy and led her to her stall.

"Lyssa is coming with us. To the mall, I mean," Christina added. "You could come, but it's turning into kind of a girl thing. . . ."

*Lyssa must be running out of turquoise fringed outfits*, Parker mused. He grinned. "It's all right." He could easily have cracked another Lyssa joke, but he had learned his lesson the first time—Christina didn't think they were funny.

Christina wandered off to find Lyssa, and Parker carried his tack into the tack room to clean it. When he came out, Christina, Lyssa, and Melanie were walking toward the outdoor ring, with Blue plodding along behind them, halterless as usual. As Parker walked up behind Blue, Parker saw that his tail was braided with feathers and bits of dark hair. Looking closer, Parker realized it was Lyssa's hair. *Whoa*, he thought.

"Hey," he called. "What's with the hair?"

The three girls turned and looked at him. Christina reached up and adjusted her ponytail. Melanie ruffled her short, blond hair. "So I stopped dying it with Kool-Aid? Get over it."

"No, I mean the hair in Blue's tail," Parker explained.

The girls were silent. "What's the big deal?" Parker persisted. "It's a fair question."

"Okay," Lyssa relented. "It's an old Native American custom. Warriors used to braid their hair into their horses' manes and tails so their spirits would be one."

Parker couldn't help it. He started to laugh.

"Sorry I asked," he said, putting his hand over his mouth to hide his smile.

A look of hurt crossed Lyssa's bright blue eyes, and Parker felt slightly guilty. But when he saw the furious look Christina shot him, he decided he wasn't sorry at all. The whole thing was ridiculous. Why couldn't Christina see that?

The girls turned their backs and walked off, their heads together, with Blue stumbling along behind them.

"She's cast a spell on them," Parker muttered. Then he climbed into his truck and roared down the driveway. For once he was glad to be heading for the library to study.

• • •

The next day when Parker showed up at Whisper-wood, Sam met him at the barn door.

"Change of plan," she said, the sun glinting off her red hair. "You and Lyssa are switching horses for the lesson."

"Sorry?"

"You'll ride Soldier Blue. Lyssa will ride Foxglove."

"Sam, I don't want to be difficult, but I don't want anyone else to ride my—," Parker started, but she cut him off.

"Relax, Parker. It can be very instructive to watch someone else ride your horse. And riding another horse will keep you on your toes."

Parker's smoky gray eyes locked with Sam's fierce green ones, and finally he looked away. He didn't want to back down, but Sam was his trainer. "Okay, fine."

As he walked down the barn aisle toward Blue's stall he smiled to himself. At least he had the easy side of the deal. Blue looked half asleep most of the time. It might be fun to wake him up and see what he could do. Parker grabbed a halter off the hook outside.

Blue was dozing when Parker unlatched his door. "Hey, big guy," Parker said, slipping into the stall.

The hulking gray regarded him with curious brown eyes. Parker was surprised when Blue allowed the halter to be slipped easily over his head. The way

Lyssa always let him walk around without it, he'd expected the horse to fight it.

After grooming him and buckling on a bridle with a big snaffle bit, Parker placed his fluffy sheepskin pad and then the saddle on Blue's back. He was just starting to do up the girth when he heard Blue let out a groan and sink to his knees. Immediately Parker undid the girth, and the horse stood up again.

"So, you're girthy, are you?" he said, rubbing the horse's chest and running his hands gently around Blue's barrel. He'd known a few horses who were extremely sensitive to the girth. His grandfather had taught him to go slowly, one hole at a time, to give the horse time to adjust.

This time the technique didn't work. Every time Parker put the buckle up a hole, the big gray started to sink.

"Hey, are you coming?" Sam called from down the aisle.

"Yeah," Parker called back. How could he admit that he hadn't been able to even to tack up Lyssa's horse?

"Need some help with that girth?"

Parker swung around as Lyssa came up behind him, leading Foxy, fully tacked and ready to go. Today she had an elaborately tooled silver barrette clipped in her hair, but the ends were floating free past her shoulders. Parker hadn't noticed how long her hair was before. Her blue eyes seemed to be twinkling in amusement.

"No," he mumbled, feeling his cheeks burn. He made one last feeble attempt, but Blue would have none of it.

Lyssa laughed lightly. "I should have warned you. He hates the girth."

"I noticed," Parker almost growled.

She handed Parker Foxy's reins, then walked over to her horse, crooning in a low, singsong voice. She ran her fingers over Blue's ears, bringing his head low, and continued talking to him. Then she straightened and went back to the girth, which she buckled tight. This time Blue didn't flinch.

"Okay, what's your secret?" Parker asked, handing back Foxy's reins.

Lyssa looked at him. "*Itancan,*" she said.

Parker rolled his eyes. "Voodoo."

"No," she said. "I just told him what I wanted. Blue needs a lot of communication. I guess he's kind of spoiled."

"Huh," Parker muttered, annoyed.

He was even more annoyed when he saw how quickly Lyssa was able to get Foxy on the bit. Her jaw was relaxed, and she moved like she was born for dressage.

On the other hand, Parker couldn't get Blue to do anything. He squeezed his legs until they were numb, but the flea-bitten gray preferred to amble and weave around the ring like an old drunk.

*Ask, tell, insist,* Parker recited to himself, calling upon the words his grandfather had used when Parker first learned to ride.

"Try talking to him," Lyssa suggested.

Parker scowled.

"It takes time," Sam said soothingly. "You have to establish a line of communication."

*It didn't take much time for Lyssa to communicate with my horse. I can't even get this guy to walk in a straight line?*

Parker bit his lip and forced himself to concentrate. There was no way he was going to let Lyssa outdo him. He tried not to nag with his hands and legs and worked at softening and communicating, asking Blue to place his feet in the same tracks every time. Finally, when the lesson was almost finished, he was able to get Blue to move off his leg. It wasn't much, but to Parker it was a victory.

"You did a good job on him," Lyssa said as they led their horses back to the barn.

*You did well on Foxy, too,* Parker wanted to respond. And it was true—Lyssa and Foxy had ridden rings around him and Blue. But somehow Parker couldn't choke out the words.

"It's not easy riding a strange horse," Lyssa added.

Parker shrugged and turned away. The fact that Lyssa was being so nice only added to his humiliation.

He felt exhausted as he led the big gray to the wash rack. Riding Blue had been a workout and a half. Lyssa followed him, leading Foxy.

"Watch out—Blue likes to act up in the wash racks," Lyssa warned.

"Don't worry," Parker scoffed. He was just bending over to grab a water bucket when he heard the whine of water running through the pipes. He looked up in time to see Blue turning on the faucet. The hose snaked across the rubber flooring and sprayed Parker in the face.

"I warned you." Lyssa laughed, ducking away from the spray. "You don't listen to anyone, do you?"

Parker grabbed the hose and turned it on Blue's back, wishing he could aim it at Lyssa instead. *Go back to Montana and leave me alone*, he wanted to yell.

6

"YOU'RE DOING WHAT?" KEVIN ASKED TWO DAYS LATER. Parker had just mounted up and was about to ride off into the woods when Kevin turned up at Whisperwood to go on a trail ride with Sam. "Schooling Foxy by yourself isn't exactly the best plan you've ever had, this close to Deer Springs and all. I mean, what about the Olympics? Don't you have to show the selection people you can, like, jump buildings and gallop for hours and stuff like that?"

"Yeah, but I'm the one riding. Sam can't qualify for me."

Kevin looked unconvinced. "I know you think you can do everything by yourself, but I still think you're better off taking lessons from a professional."

*Except that all she's been teaching is what she learned*

*from the Cowgirl of the Plains,* Parker thought sourly. But he couldn't exactly say that to Kevin about his half sister. Parker looked away from his friend. *I just wish everyone would stop trying to tell me what to do.*

"Don't worry, I'll be fine. Have a good trail ride, Kev." With that, Parker rode off through the trees toward a secluded clearing he'd discovered last summer. The ground was flat, and the footing was good. He could work Foxy without interference.

Starting out slowly, Parker worked Foxy on a tight circle at a walk and then at a collected sitting trot. But as soon as he asked for the working canter, he felt it again. Foxy wasn't engaged from behind.

"It's so basic," Parker muttered. Gritting his teeth, he drove harder with his seat bones. "Please listen, Foxy," he pleaded. "You *do* want to go to the Olympics, don't you?"

Foxy tossed her head, not a good sign. "I guess our spirit is not one today," Parker scoffed. Suddenly he had a crazy idea. Looking around to make sure no one was watching, he tugged out a couple of strands of his dark hair. Then he dismounted and knotted them into Foxy's tail.

"I can't believe I just did that," Parker said to his mare as he climbed back into the saddle.

Feeling foolish, he laughed aloud. Then he settled back to work at the sitting trot, frowning in concentration. A few minutes later he cued her to canter once more, squeezing forcefully with his outside leg. This time Foxy bucked. *So much for Lyssa's ancient customs*, Parker thought, giving up.

He turned Foxy to pop over a few fallen logs piled up at the edge of the clearing. They were positioned so that he could jump them in figure eights, turning tighter and more quickly each time. Foxy came alive, turning lightly as a cat, always leaving from a perfect distance. After a few rounds Parker circled her wide and once again asked for the working canter. This time Foxy did it right, tucking her hind end under and engaging from behind. For the first time that day Parker smiled. It was a small victory, and they still had a long way to go, but it was a start.

"Good girl," Parker praised, bringing Foxy to a halt and patting her neck. Foxy took a couple of extra steps, rolling her eyes toward a rustling in the trees.

Suddenly Parker heard a twig snap, and Foxy whickered as Lyssa rode out of the clump of trees. Riding bareback and bridleless as usual, her hands were laced in Blue's mane, and she was blushing.

"Sorry, I was just riding by, and I couldn't help watching. I didn't mean to interrupt, but Blue wanted to say hello to Foxy."

Parker tried to appear calm, but he was seething.

"I'd rather you didn't," he said icily. "I rode out here to be alone."

Lyssa nodded and nudged Blue with her heels. "I know. But I'm not sorry I watched. I learned something from you today."

Parker watched her ride off, wishing he knew a few magic tricks himself. He'd have liked to put a hex or whatever they called it on that prying cowgirl from Montana!

Later that week Parker bumped into Sam on his way into the barn

"I'm glad to see you're plugging away at your dressage, even if you're doing it solo," Sam said.

*Lyssa told her,* Parker thought instantly.

"Yeah, well," Parker said, avoiding Sam's gaze. "I think we're getting somewhere."

He hoped that Sam wasn't offended. It was easier this way—and it kept him from hearing about Lyssa every five minutes. It was bad enough that since she was working on the farm, he kept bumping into her everywhere. Christina was at Whisperwood all the time now, too, hanging out with Lyssa. So Parker had to avoid her, too.

Parker watched as Sam continued on the path

before leading Foxy into an empty paddock to roll. Foxy ambled away, head down, sniffing the bluegrass until she found the perfect place to roll. After she had gotten herself good and dirty, she stood up and shook herself off, blinking lazily in the sun. Parker walked over and stroked her finely chiseled head. He squinted, noticing Christina sitting on an overturned bucket two paddocks over. She was watching Lyssa, who appeared to be trying to lead a big bay up a set of steps.

Parker shaded his eyes, then walked over to get a closer look.

"Hi," Christina whispered, not looking up.

"What's she doing with Wildcat?" Parker whispered back.

"Training him. Check this out. It's amazing," Christina said excitedly. "I've learned so much from her."

Now that Parker was closer, he could see that Lyssa was encouraging Wildcat to walk up a series of stairs made out of some stacked railroad ties. At first the big warmblood snorted and backed up, but finally, with Lyssa's encouragement, he placed a tentative hoof on the first step, and Lyssa praised him lavishly.

Parker snorted. "I don't see what's so amazing about that. If she was teaching him to *jump* the steps, that would make sense."

"Shhh. I'm trying to watch. Sit down. Maybe you'll learn something," Christina hissed.

"Okay, I give up. What exactly are you learning? How is forcing some poor horse to walk up steps going to make you a better jockey?"

Christina shook her head. "Don't you see? It's not about *steps*. It's about making horses understand that there's no reason they can't do anything. It makes them feel more confident when they encounter any obstacle, on the track or on a cross-country course."

"Did Lyssa tell you that?"

Christina's eyes flashed fire. "Yeah," she said. "And I think she has a point. Her methods sure seem to work."

"I prefer the methods we've always used—pretty successfully, I might add," Parker said quietly.

"Okay," Christina agreed. "But it can't hurt to learn new things."

Parker kicked at the ground with his toe. Why was it was becoming harder and harder to talk to Christina? All they did was fight, about Lyssa.

*Only two more weeks until Deer Springs, and Lyssa will pack up that ratty trailer of hers and disappear,* he thought with relief. But the relief was short-lived. In a few short weeks he'd have a pretty good idea if he was going to be selected for the Olympic team. There was so much to do.

"See you later," Parker said, turning to bring Foxy in. He could feel Christina's eyes bore into his back all the way back to the paddock.

"How'd it go?" Sam asked the following day.

Parker had just ridden over the advanced cross-country course that he'd helped Sam and Tor build at Whisperwood.

"Great," Parker lied, pulling off his helmet and pushing back his sweaty hair as he rode up to where Sam was standing in the stable yard, waving goodbye to some of her students. Then he let out his breath in an explosive whoosh. "Well, not great. Foxy's gotten into the habit of leaning on her forehand. I felt like we were riding downhill over the whole course."

Sam reached over to adjust the noseband on Foxy's bridle. "Sounds like you need to bring her weight back."

"Sometimes I can do it. It's just not consistent. I've tried everything."

"It's called dressage. Dressage and more dressage. Working by yourself is great, but you might want to consider another session with me."

"Okay, sure," Parker said, pulling off his gloves.

"Don't be too discouraged," Sam said. "You've made it this far."

Parker tucked his helmet under his arm and led

Foxy around in small circles. "I know," he said tiredly. "It just seems like I can't move on."

Sam looked at him thoughtfully. "You're going after an awfully big prize. It's easy to psyched yourself out. You need to change your patterns a bit and relax a little more. After you put Foxy away, why don't you come over to the indoor arena? Lyssa and I set up some barrels."

*Oh no, not Lyssa again,* Parker thought. "What for?" he asked.

"You'll see," Sam said mysteriously.

"All right."

Parker sponged Foxy off with warm, soapy water, then rubbed her legs with alcohol to brace them. After he put her in her stall, he wandered over to the indoor arena. The last thing he wanted was to watch Lyssa's tricks, but he'd told Sam he would.

From his position by the in gate he could see that Lyssa had placed three barrels at even distances around the arena. She was mounted on Blue, who was wearing a big western saddle. Lyssa's long legs were wrapped around Blue's barrel, and she was crouching low over his neck, galloping in and out of the barrels in a cloverleaf pattern.

"Barrel racing?" Parker asked in disbelief as Sam came up beside him.

Sam laughed. "Unconventional, I know, but Lyssa

swears by it. All that bending and turning keeps Blue's weight back and helps him stay engaged when he's jumping."

"You want me to try barrel racing?" Parker asked, shaking his head. "No way."

"Just watch," Sam advised.

Blue ran around the last barrel, thundered down the center line, and skidded to a stop, his hindquarters tucked neatly under him, right in front of Sam and Parker.

Lyssa's eyes sparkled, and her cheeks were flushed. "We haven't raced barrels in ages," she said happily, patting Blue's neck.

"Looks like fun," Sam said.

The girl nodded enthusiastically. "You bet. And Blue really has to use himself to get around the barrels. Of course, he likes working cattle better."

"Want me to go round up a cow or two for him?" Parker asked sarcastically.

Lyssa frowned, then wheeled Blue around and galloped off for another go at the barrels.

"Parker, what's eating you?" Sam demanded. "That was rude, and I always thought you were so polite."

Parker hung his head. "I'm sorry. I'm not really myself these days. Nerves, I guess."

Sam got a funny look on her face, then turned back

to watch Lyssa and Blue scramble around the barrels. "You know, you might very well end up on the Olympic team with Lyssa," she said softly.

Parker couldn't say anything. He really hadn't thought about that.

"Which means she'll be your *teammate*," Sam said.

"So?"

"So, the Olympic committee is big on individual talent, of course, but there's a lot of talent out there to choose from. They're looking for people with the ability to work together for the greater good of the team."

Her eyes never left Parker's face.

"So you think I need to be more of a team player?" Parker asked hesitantly.

"I knew you were more than just a handsome face," Sam said, beaming at him.

But Parker didn't feel like smiling. "Okay," he said after a pause. "So I need to be more of a team player. But if you ask me, Lyssa needs to get serious and stop asking for attention with her rodeo tricks."

He didn't stop to hear Sam's reply. Instead he walked away and headed for his truck. Even the cool reception he knew he'd get at Townsend Acres from his parents would be preferable to having Lyssa shoved in his face every time he turned around.

Over the next few days Parker continued schooling

Foxy on his own. Soon, however, Parker began to dread his solitary sessions. Some days he'd take Foxy to the clearing in the woods and work her over cavalletti poles. Other days he'd gallop over the cross-country course. But no matter how hard he worked, he and Foxy didn't seem to get anywhere.

Sitting in his room on Sunday evening, Parker considered his dilemma. It wasn't Foxy's fault. He was riding badly. He looked at a silver-framed picture of his grandfather thoughtfully. Clay was an incredible horseman. He'd left his number in Ireland just in case of an emergency. *Well, this is an emergency*, Parker decided as he picked up the phone.

"Yes?"

Parker smiled to hear the beloved gravelly voice of Clay Townsend.

"Grandfather? It's Parker. I need your help."

"Oh, dear," Clay said. "Is this about your father?"

"Actually, that's not the problem," Parker said. He cleared his throat, feeling awkward. "It's Foxy, or rather, me. I feel like everything we've been working for is falling apart, and I don't have any time to waste."

Parker explained the events of the last couple of weeks, tearing Lyssa to pieces but leaving out the fact that he was schooling by himself.

When he paused, Clay replied, "I don't understand. Sam is a top instructor. What does she say?"

Parker toyed with the phone cord. He didn't want to admit that he'd stopped listening to Sam. "She says I should just relax—and take a few more dressage lessons with her."

"Sounds like pretty reasonable advice to me. Let me leave you with one parting thought I learned from an old horseman I admired named Jimmy Williams, who won Horseman of the Year back in the sixties. His favorite line was, 'It's what you learn about riding after you think you know everything that counts.' "

*Whatever that means*, Parker thought.

After he hung up the phone, he flopped onto his bed and looked out his window at the night sky. He was disappointed. Normally Parker listened to every word his grandfather said, but this time he made no sense. If only there was someone else he could talk to.

Not his father—Brad would simply give him the same old line about giving up eventing and concentrating on the family business.

There was always Christina, but she had made it very clear that Lyssa could do no wrong. *I might as well forget talking to her till Lyssa leaves*, Parker thought dismally.

Which left Sam. She was his teacher, after all. There was no getting around it.

• • •

The next day Parker stopped by Sam's office. She looked up from her desk, which was piled high with papers.

"Hi," Parker said sheepishly.

"Hi," Sam answered with a smile, as if the problems of the last few days had never happened.

"Sorry about skipping lessons—and everything," he said. He scanned her face anxiously, trying to gauge her reaction.

Sam closed up a folder and reached for another one. "No problem. I miss teaching you, but as long as you're doing the work, it doesn't matter how you do it. I gather that all's going well?"

"That's just it," Parker said. "It's not going well. Foxy and I are all out of sync. I can't put my finger on it."

Sam leaned forward. "Maybe you need to take a break," she said.

"How can I take time off? Deer Springs is so soon—"

"I don't mean stop riding. I just mean when you're not schooling Foxy, go have some fun. What have you been doing for relaxation lately?"

"Relaxation? Uh—running, working out, studying, I guess."

"Not exactly relaxing," Sam said. "You need to go have some fun, and don't think about horses or competing. Take Christina out."

92

"Well, I am supposed to take her to the fall dance at the high school," Parker said.

"That's a start, but do something else. Right now. Tonight."

As Parker drove back to Townsend Acres he decided Sam was right. He had gotten way too preoccupied with schooling and worrying about being selected for the Olympics. He needed a change of scene.

After dinner he phoned Christina.

"Hi, Parker," Christina answered the phone breathlessly. She sounded like she was in a good mood.

"Listen, I haven't really had a chance to talk to you in a while. How about I pick you up and we can go see a movie or something?"

Christina sighed. "I can't, Parker, sorry. I asked Lyssa over to dinner, and we're just sitting down to eat."

Parker frowned. "Well, then, how about tomorrow night? I could meet you at Whitebrook."

"I'm sorry, but I've already made plans. Lyssa's coming to watch me work Star, then afterward we're going to meet some of her friends who're in for a team-roping competition or something."

Parker frowned. "Lyssa again, huh?"

"What's wrong with that?" Christina demanded.

"You've been spending so much time with her

lately. Have you forgotten about your friends?"

"I don't know what's wrong with you lately, Parker. These last few days you've been avoiding me, and suddenly you pop up, expecting me to drop everything to be with you."

"That's not fair," Parker shot back. "I haven't been avoiding you. In case you've forgotten, it takes a little work to qualify for the Olympics."

There was a long pause before Christina spoke, more softly this time. "You know, Parker, sometimes you act like you're the only one who's got dreams. Why is it okay for you to be busy but not okay for me?"

Parker was about to reply, but he slammed down the phone instead. He stood there, staring at it stupidly. He'd never felt more alone in his life.

*You're some team player, Parker Townsend,* he thought miserably.

**7**

*I OUGHT TO SAY HI,* PARKER THOUGHT AS HE WATCHED Christina and Lyssa climb into Lyssa's beat-up truck in the Whisperwood parking area on Thursday afternoon. He'd just driven up, and Foxy was inside, waiting to be ridden. But instead of getting out of his truck, Parker leaned down as if he were searching for something on the floor. He had to remain in that position for a while because Lyssa's truck kept stalling, but finally he heard the truck cough to life and sputter away down the drive.

"I can't believe I did that," Parker mumbled as he started across the yard toward Foxy's stall. It had been like that all week—Parker had been hiding from Christina and Lyssa. But it was better than quarreling all the time, Parker told himself.

*I'll smooth things over with her when I pick her up for the fall dance tomorrow,* Parker thought while he was riding. But then a thought struck him. Christina was still planning on going with him, wasn't she?

That night Parker decided he'd better call to make sure.

"Hello, Parker." Christina's voice was cool, and Parker took a deep breath before continuing in a rush.

"So, what time should I pick you up for the dance?"

"Well," Christina said, "I won't be finished with my barn chores until five, and I'll need time to get ready. Six-thirty?"

"Great," Parker said, relieved that they were still on.

It was only afterward that he realized he hadn't asked her what color dress she was wearing so he could order a corsage to match. Well, he'd think of something.

He wandered down to the kitchen, opened the refrigerator, and grabbed a carton of milk.

"Oh, Parker, let me do that for you," said Connie, scurrying in. In a flash she poured the milk into a crystal jug and set out a glass for him. "I just made fresh blueberry muffins."

*Yum,* Parker thought, realizing how nice it was to be around someone who was always kind to him no matter what.

"You ready for that big event of yours?" Connie asked as she placed a plate of muffins in front of him.

"As ready as I'll ever be."

"Well, my husband and I are looking forward to seeing you in the Olympics." She lowered her voice. "I don't care what Mr. and Mrs. Townsend say."

"Thanks," Parker said through a mouthful of muffin. He gave the old woman a grateful hug. "These muffins are great, by the way."

Connie was about to leave the kitchen when Parker had an idea.

"Uh, I have a question for you. If you're going to take a girl to a dance and you need to order a corsage and you don't know what color dress she's wearing, what should you do?"

"You should call the girl and ask her," Connie said, as if it were perfectly obvious. She peered at Parker. "Are you having problems with Christina?"

Parker shook his head, but he knew she wasn't convinced.

Connie paused in the doorway as she left the room. "White rosebuds," she called over her shoulder. "They'll go with anything."

"Thanks. You're the best," Parker called after her.

The next afternoon, after he'd schooled Foxy, Parker drove to town. He had just enough time to pick up Christina's wrist corsage at the florist.

As he walked into the little shop he saw Kevin standing at the counter, paying for a spray of tiny pink rosebuds in a plastic box.

"First it was Dylan and now you. I'm bumping into practically everyone we know here today," Kevin said when Parker walked up to the counter next to him.

"Who is that for?"

Kevin picked up the box and looked uncomfortable. He tossed back his wavy auburn hair and shrugged. "Well, I wish it was for Melanie, but she's going with some other guy."

Parker nodded. "Yeah, I heard."

"So I'm taking Lindsay Devereaux."

"I don't think I've ever met her," Parker said.

"She's the sister of one of the guys on my baseball team," Kevin explained.

"Well, good," Parker said. "I'm glad you're going." He inspected the corsage he'd ordered for Christina. White rosebuds nestled in greenery with baby's breath thrown in for good measure. They were pretty. Thank goodness for Connie.

"See ya at the gym," Kevin said as he turned to leave.

Parker watched him go, feeling a little sad. At one time they'd have all gone to the dance together, in Parker's truck. They might have gone out for a nice dinner beforehand. But that was before Melanie and

Kevin had broken up. Now things were different.

Different *is the word, all right,* Parker thought that evening as he drove from Whitebrook to the gym at Henry Clay. Christina had hardly said a word to him yet.

"I like your dress," Parker said, trying to make conversation. "Red is your color."

"Thanks," Christina said, smoothing her hair and turning away from him to look out the window.

Parker scanned his brain, trying to think of something to say, but he couldn't think of anything that wouldn't somehow lead to the dreaded topic of Lyssa.

"Can you believe how cold it's getting already?" he asked. The weather was usually a safe subject, although it wasn't that cold at all. In fact, the windows were down, and the breeze felt nice on his face.

Christina looked at him. "Not really."

Parker rolled his eyes in the darkness. Now they were disagreeing about the weather. *This is way too weird,* Parker thought. Usually when he and Christina were together, they couldn't stop talking about horses and racing and . . . everything. *Will it ever be the same between us?* he wondered as he turned into the school parking lot.

Across the lot Parker saw Kevin awkwardly open the door for a tall, blond girl he supposed was Lindsay. As they walked down the hall ahead of Parker and

Christina, Parker noticed how much space was between them. When Kevin had been going out with Melanie, they always held hands.

He and Christina weren't going to break up, he told himself firmly, taking her arm. And they were going to have a good time tonight no matter what.

"Ready, Chris?" he asked, flashing his most dazzling smile.

"Ready," Christina said, her voice tight.

Together they entered the gym. Red, white, and black balloons covered the ceiling, and colorful lights bounced off the walls.

Christina leaned close to Parker. "I can't believe this is my last year here," she said.

Parker was so thrilled to hear her say something, he didn't think about his response. "So what are you thinking about college?"

Christina pressed her lips together. "If anyone asks me anything more about college, I'll scream."

Instantly Parker drew back, sorry that he'd touched on a sensitive spot. He remembered all too clearly how he'd felt his senior year. His dad had pressured him like crazy to go to school in Italy when he wanted to stay home and continue his riding career. Everyone gave him advice, all of it conflicting. He knew it was the same for Christina.

"Sorry, I—I—," Christina stuttered.

"Never mind. I shouldn't have asked."

"My head is totally spinning," Christina went. "I've been so busy with Star, I haven't really thought about it that much." She glanced over at Melanie, who was talking and laughing with Jeff Harper. "Mel seems to have it all figured out. She wants to take a few years off, become a famous jockey, then retire and go to art school. I want to be a famous jockey, too, but I still want to go to college."

Parker put his hand on her shoulder. "You'll figure it out. You always do."

Christina shrugged, but she looked worried. Parker was angry with himself. He had to find some way to cheer her up.

"Hey, look. There's Dylan and Katie," Parker said with forced enthusiasm. "Let's go say hi."

As the evening went on, Parker found that he wasn't his usual party self. Ordinarily he tended to gather his friends around him and make jokes to keep them entertained. Tonight he couldn't think of a single funny line. Instead he sat with Christina at a small table at the edge of the dance floor and observed his friends.

Kevin seemed to be having a good time with Lindsay, and Parker was glad. But Kevin kept glancing over at where Melanie was dancing with Jeff. "Don't worry. That's not going anywhere," Christina had said, following Parker's gaze. "Jeff isn't into horses; Mel could never be serious about him."

"Hmmm," Parker replied, hoping that was true. "I can't get used to seeing her and Kevin apart, though."

"Me too," Christina said, gazing at him steadily. "You think something will last forever, but then it doesn't work out."

Parker felt his blood run cold. What was she hinting at? That maybe he and she weren't working out? Christina was gazing across the room, tapping her feet to the music. Parker studied her face, but he couldn't tell what she was thinking.

"Christina?" Parker blurted out. "Were you implying that maybe *we* weren't working out?"

Christina whirled around to face him, her eyes narrowed. "Why, is that what you think?" she demanded.

"No. Not at all. I'm sorry," Parker muttered, and slumped back in his chair. He was so confused. He should have never said anything.

He waited anxiously for Christina to say something else to smooth the tension, but she didn't appear to want to talk anymore. So they sat in silence.

"Do you want to dance?" Parker asked after a while. He didn't feel like dancing, but he didn't want Christina to be bored, either.

Christina shook her head. "Not now."

Parker shifted uncomfortably in his chair. Was

Christina really angry enough to consider breaking up with him?

"Good night, Parker," Christina said coolly when they got to Whitebrook.

Without even waiting for Parker to get out of the truck and come around to open her door, Christina jumped out and strode up to the door of the farmhouse.

*At least she could have waved,* Parker thought sadly.

On Sunday morning Parker headed into Whisperwood's tack room to grab Foxy's saddle and bridle. Lyssa had gotten there ahead of him. Her dark hair was in a thick French braid tied off with Blue's gray hair.

*She's taking this one-with-my-horse thing a little too far,* Parker thought disparagingly.

Lyssa looked up from the big western saddle she was soaping. "Have a good time at the dance?"

Parker nodded and grabbed his bridle off the rack.

"Wasn't Christina's dress beautiful? She was hoping you'd like it."

Parker grunted. He was in no mood to strike up a conversation with Lyssa about Christina, or anything, for that matter. It was her fault that things were going so badly. Hurriedly he grabbed his saddle and took off.

After mucking out Foxy's stall and grooming her,

Parker realized he'd grabbed Kaitlin's bridle by mistake. He went back to the tack room. Lyssa had finished cleaning her saddle and was now oiling it.

"Want me to clean your tack after the lesson?" she asked. "You know, we have it together today."

"Fine," he said carelessly. He wished he could work Foxy by himself, but he couldn't run out on Sam, not this close to Deer Springs. Besides, Lyssa might be his future teammate. He was stuck with her.

Parker retrieved his bridle, watching Lyssa out of the corner of his eye. He wondered if she knew how much she annoyed him. If so, she didn't show it. She screwed the top back on the neat's-foot-oil can, humming all the while.

"Why do you bother cleaning saddles when you hardly ever ride in them?" he asked.

"Why do you bother worrying about what I do?" Lyssa shot back.

Parker glared at her, then left to tack up Foxy. Leading the mare out of the barn and into the sunshine, he mounted up and headed her toward the cross-country field.

They were just warming up with some figure eights at the trot when Lyssa and Blue came jogging up the path. Parker stayed out of her way as she walked Blue in a big circle. A few minutes later Sam appeared.

"What a beautiful day," she said conversationally.

"All right, let's get to work. Deer Springs is the toughest event either of you have faced, and you've got to be prepared."

"Tell me about it," Parker said, setting his jaw. He was eager to start jumping, and Foxy felt full of herself and ready to go.

"Let's start with a couple of brush fences," Sam said. "Remember, focus on communication. Use your seat, your hands, and your legs effectively, and the rest will fall into place. Lyssa, go ahead and start."

Lyssa clucked and sent Blue into a canter toward the first fence. Even without a bridle and saddle, she looked cool and collected. Having ridden Blue, Parker knew he wasn't easy. But the hulking gray took the brush and then a big rolltop with smooth, even strides and cantered on to the next set of fences without mishap.

Parker followed. He missed the distance to the brush, rushing Foxy so she had to add a stride at the last minute. They were crooked going to the rolltop, and Foxy peeked at it, jumping it long and landing with a buck.

*Get it together*, Parker thought as they continued on, jumping over a ditch and heading toward the hayrack. He tried losing himself in the rhythm of Foxy's stride, but he still felt stiff. He could barely face Sam after such a disappointing performance.

"You're riding defensively," Sam said when he had halted in front of her. "Let them rest a second, and then let's try the water jump."

"I hope you don't mind me saying this," Lyssa said while Sam went over to adjust something at the water jump. "But I think you could fix what's throwing Foxy off by giving her a little more support just before your takeoffs."

Parker stared at her coldly. Lyssa hesitated but went on. "I don't mean kicking her or anything; I mean—"

"I know what you mean," Parker said loudly. "You think everyone wants to hear what you think. Well, guess what? I don't, O Great *Itancan*."

Lyssa's cheeks stained bright red. "I'm just trying to help."

Parker cut her off. "You barged in here with your horse whisperer tricks, thinking you know more about horses than anyone."

"I don't think I know more than anyone else," Lyssa said calmly.

"Just mind your own business, will you?"

"Parker, that's enough!" Sam called.

Parker twisted in his saddle to see Sam come up behind him, her face like a thundercloud.

"Nerves are no excuse for this sort of rudeness. You owe Lyssa an apology," she commanded sternly.

"*I* should apologize? But—," Parker began.

Lyssa began to laugh, and Parker glared at her once more. Her musical laugh set Parker off more than anything else about her. "Don't worry about it, Sam. No offense taken," she said. And with that, she trotted off.

Gritting his teeth, Parker turned Foxy in the opposite direction. He'd show Lyssa what he thought of her and her advice. Squeezing his legs, he urged Foxy into a gallop and turned her toward the water jump.

"Parker, don't make things worse. Pull up and cool off!" Sam ordered. "I mean it. Slow down, Parker!"

But Parker galloped on. At the last minute he tried to pull back as he realized how fast they were going. Foxy's head was up, and her stride was choppy. She'd never make it over. But by some miracle she managed to gather herself and clear it, landing awkwardly on the other side in the water and stumbling. Parker was thrown up on her neck, and as the mare tried to regain her footing and scramble for the opposite bank, he tumbled into the water. Foxy heaved herself forward, and just in time to avoid being dragged, Parker let go of the reins, sinking in the muddy quagmire.

*This isn't happening*, he thought as his face hit the water.

He was dimly aware of a voice. He sat up in the muddy water, sputtering and trying to get his bearings.

"Parker, you okay? Raise your hand if you can hear me," Lyssa called anxiously as she rode over.

Parker closed his eyes, humiliation seeping into every pore of his being. Shakily he stood up, swiping at the mud in his eyes as he scanned the area for Foxy.

The mare had stopped a little ways off, and she stood regarding Parker with liquid brown eyes. He sloshed his way over to her and dropped to his knees, feeling every inch of her legs.

"Are you all right, girl?" he asked over and over.

Sam walked over and knelt down next to him.

Parker stiffened. "I know, you don't have to say it. It was a stupid, stupid thing to do."

"Go get cleaned off, Parker," Sam said quietly.

Parker stalked back to the barn with Foxy in tow. He kept his eyes down to avoid catching anyone's gaze. It was bad enough that he'd fallen right in front of Lyssa and Sam. He didn't want to explain his mud-soaked clothes to anyone else.

8

"I'M SO SORRY, GIRL," PARKER SAID AS HE LED FOXY PAST the farrier's truck that was parked in the stable area. *If anything's happened to her, I'll never forgive myself*, he thought, stopping Foxy just in front of the barn aisle. Leaning over, he ran his hands over her legs once more, then scanned the rest of her body. After a fall like that, he couldn't believe Foxy wasn't injured. He jogged her up and down the stable area to see if she favored one of her legs, but she moved out as soundly as ever.

Stroking Foxy's mud-streaked coat and looking into the liquid depths of her eyes, Parker wondered if this crash had stirred up the memory of their crash at Meadowlark. Parker had never forgotten it, but he was sure Foxy had. For the hundredth time since it had happened, the scene flashed before Parker's eyes. Foxy bobbled at a large hay manger that they weren't supposed to jump in the first place. Parker remembered the blinding pain he'd felt when Foxy landed on top of him and the insufferable guilt when he found out Foxy had a bone chip in her hock. He had nearly ended both of their careers before they even got started.

And today he'd nearly done it again.

Clipping Foxglove into the crossties, Parker began to pull off her dirty tack. Why hadn't he listened to Sam when she'd told him to stop? Why didn't he listen to anyone, ever?

Something he'd overheard Lyssa telling Christina recently came to mind. It was an old Cherokee saying: "Listen! Or your tongue will make you deaf."

"Talk about deaf," Parker scolded himself angrily as he struggled to unbuckle Foxy's girth. She nuzzled him trustingly.

"You deserve a case of Polos for putting up with me," he mumbled, burying his face in her mane.

As Parker pulled off the soggy saddle he felt like he was moving in slow motion. It was going to take hours to clean and oil the saddle. He'd have to use a toothpick to dig the mud out from all the cracks and crevices. If he didn't get to work right away, the mud would dry and crack the leather.

But he had to give Foxy a warm bath. He peeled off his fleece jacket, wincing when pain shot through his shoulder. He led Foxy to the wash rack, groaning as he filled a bucket with warm water. He'd probably pulled a muscle.

*Serves you right,* Parker thought savagely.

The worst part was that a successful event rider depended on the complete trust of their mount. Since a horse wasn't allowed to see the cross-country course before jumping it, the horse relied on the rider's judgment. And Foxy had every right not to trust Parker now.

Lost as he was in his depressing thoughts, Parker didn't pay any attention as Chad Barrett, the blacksmith, walked up to fill a bucket with cold water. He turned on the hose, studying Foxy's feet.

"Something's loose down there. I'll take a look at her after I've finished with the others," Chad said, shutting off the water. "You'd better put her on the board just before Deer Springs. I'm getting pretty booked up."

Parker nodded silently, glad when the blacksmith left, laughing at something as he strode down the aisle. Parker watched the muddy water flow down the drain, and suddenly it hit him—maybe everyone was laughing at him. Maybe it was obvious to everyone but him that there was no way he'd ever make the Olympic combined-training team. If his mediocre riding over the last few weeks had been a question mark, his fall today had been the exclamation point.

*You're not good enough, Parker Townsend.*

"Is that you, Parker? Oh, dear, look at our son." Lavinia's voice pierced the air.

Parker whirled around to see his mother and father gliding down the aisle in their self-important way. Brad, in his one of his signature blue blazers, Lavinia in shiny alligator pumps—her barn shoes.

*Oh, great, this is just what I need,* Parker thought, wondering what on earth had brought them to Whisperwood today of all days.

"What happened to you?" Lavinia giggled. "Did that little horse of yours trip over herself?"

"It was my fault," Parker said, bending low to sponge off Foxy's wide barrel. He wished desperately that his parents would disappear. There was an awkward pause. Brad eyed Foxy distastefully.

"Aren't you going to ask us why we're here?" Lavinia asked.

Parker rolled his eyes. "Why are you here, Mother?" he asked through clenched teeth. "Maybe you heard about my fall and you wanted to come and rub it in?"

"Don't talk to your mother that way," Brad thundered.

Lavinia sighed dramatically. "This is what happens

when we let you hang around the barn all the time with all these . . . people," she said with disgust.

"There's nothing wrong with the people here," Parker said defensively.

"Have you seen that awful cowgirl Samantha has hanging around?" Lavinia demanded, turning to Brad. "June Talbot was telling me all about the horrible outfits she parades around in. Turquoise suede pantsuits?"

Brad laughed, clearly amused.

Parker bristled. Sure, he might not be Lyssa's number-one fan, but he couldn't stand hearing his parents put her down. They were such snobs.

"What's wrong with that 'cowgirl,' as you call her?" he flashed. "She happens to be a fine rider, and she knows horses better than all three of us put together." As he stood up to face his parents a chunk of mud fell from his cheek and rolled across the wet rubber mat on the floor of the wash rack.

Brad looked at it, shaking his head.

"Really, Parker. Why don't you get a groom to clean up that horse of yours and go take a shower? You're covered with mud—and you're embarrassing your mother and me," he said sharply.

"So sorry," Parker choked out, angry tears blurring his vision as he turned back to Foxy. But he knew better than to try and argue.

"We came here because we never see you around the house anymore," began Lavinia. "But we've made a decision, and we wanted to talk to you about it."

"It's too late if you're planning to send me away to boarding school again. In case you forgot, I've already graduated from high school. I'm at the University of Kentucky now, remember?"

Brad's eyes narrowed. "Don't smart-mouth me, son. This little Olympic dream of yours; it's all very thrilling, I'm sure. But look at yourself. Do you really think you should be going after something that's not only beneath you but obviously beyond your talents as well?"

Parker stepped back as if he'd been punched in the stomach. *That's exactly what I've been thinking.*

Brad cleared his throat and went on, with Lavinia looking smug beside him. "This . . . eventing is a crude form of riding. All yee-haw and hurl yourself over a few logs as fast as you can. It's all right for that cowgirl, but it's not the sort of thing a Townsend ought to be doing."

"I don't know who you people are, but I think you're way wrong!"

Parker froze as Lyssa's voice reached his ears. Had she been there the whole time? Had she heard everything? He whirled around to see Lyssa, glaring at his parents with stormy blue eyes.

114

"Uh, Lyssa," Parker said slowly. "These are my parents."

Lyssa blinked and folded her arms over her chest.

"Well, they're not *my* parents, so I don't have to stand there and listen to all their . . . *hooey* like you do, Parker," she said, glancing at him.

"What a very *large* belt buckle," Lavinia said in a syrupy voice. "Is that a real sapphire?"

"It is, and I won it. I really don't care if you think I dress weird. Where I come from, people's characters are more important than what they wear."

"Lyssa, she didn't mean it," Parker began.

Lyssa tossed her head, her thick braid flopping over her shoulder. "Let me finish." She turned to Brad. "I don't know where you get off crushing Parker's dreams, but I think you're unfair and ignorant. Do you know how hard it is to be an Olympic contender?"

"Are you speaking to me, young lady?" Brad sneered.

"Well, *duh*," Lyssa retorted.

In spite of everything, Parker had to stifle a laugh. Few people had ever spoken to Brad like that before. He had to hand it to Lyssa—she had guts.

"I don't know Parker all that well," Lyssa continued. "But he's got what it takes. You're his folks. You ought to help him, not stand in his way. Have you seen how he handles that mare? I've ridden her, and she's talented, but she's a handful. Parker has a gift—he's *good*."

Parker's jaw dropped. After the horrible way he'd treated her, Lyssa was defending him?

"And another thing. For your information, eventing is based on the military training that cavalry horses needed for war. It requires bravery and heart in horse and rider. It's part of our history, and I don't think you have any right to criticize it!"

"Right out of a textbook. Bravo," said Lavinia sarcastically.

Lyssa glared at her. "I'm going to the Olympics, and nothing's going to stop me." She glanced at Parker. "Parker's like me, whether he knows it or not. When we're at the Olympics, people like you will be sitting in the stands, wishing you had the guts to go after your dreams!"

Angry tears spilled down Lyssa's cheeks. She turned and rushed down the aisle to the tack room.

Lavinia sniffed loudly and looked at Parker with contempt.

"Your new friend is so . . . passionate about her beliefs," she said with a forced smile.

"She was completely out of line," Brad huffed.

Parker unclipped Foxy and led her into the aisle. "If you'll excuse me, I have work to do," he said coldly, leading Foxy away.

His head was spinning with everything he'd just heard. Maybe he had something to learn from Lyssa after all: *Never let anyone stand in the way of your dreams.*

Parker was just putting Foxy back in her stall when his father came up behind him, alone.

"You owe your mother an apology," Brad said sharply.

Parker stared at his father in amazement. "Actually, I think you both owe *me* an apology."

He waited for the explosion that he was sure would follow, but instead Brad opened his mouth and shut it before turning and walking away, his shoulders slumped.

"Parker finally wins a round," Parker whispered, leaning wearily against Foxy.

When he considered his losses lately, it had to count for *something*.

9

"No problem. You know where the towels are, and there's a stack of clean laundry on the washing machine. You ought to find something that fits," said Tor, looking up from a manure spreader he was trying to repair. His expression hadn't changed a bit when Parker approached and sheepishly asked if he could use the Nelsons' shower and borrow a change of clothes.

"Thanks," Parker said quickly.

Parker let the warm water smooth out the knots in his shoulders and relax his aching muscles. Afterward he pulled on a T-shirt that said Devon Grand Prix, a pair of Tor's faded jeans, and an old pair of sneakers.

Parker was just walking down the hall when he passed the room he'd stayed in when he'd lived with the Nelsons. He couldn't resist. Opening the door, he looked inside, startled by the room's transformation. Instead of the faded blue comforter that had always been on the bed, there was a multicolored Navajo blanket. Two pairs of cowboy boots were lined up at the foot of the bed, next to a turquoise duffel bag with the monogram LH. On the little side table Parker saw a framed photograph. Walking over, he picked it up and studied it. A younger Lyssa and a suntanned man sat bareback on a palomino horse. A laughing woman with eyes like Lyssa's was holding the reins.

*Is that Lyssa's mom and dad?* Parker peered more closely.

Suddenly he realized he was snooping, and he slipped hurriedly out of the room.

Parker tossed his rolled-up clothes in the bed of his truck and returned to the barn. Then he picked up his muddy saddle and bridle and carried them into the tack room.

"What a nightmare. It'll be a miracle if this leather doesn't crack," Parker muttered as he began the tedious process of taking apart his bridle piece by piece, looping them over the metal bridle hook hanging from the ceiling. "And I've made a mess out of everything else as well," he added under his breath.

Moodily Parker rolled up his sleeves and swiped at a bar of glycerin soap with a damp tack sponge. He began to clean his bridle, deep in thought.

It was all very well to admire Lyssa's determination, but she and Blue were going well. He and Foxy were another matter.

*Time to face facts, Townsend,* Parker told himself sternly. If he rode as badly as he had over the past few weeks, there was no way the Olympic committee would choose him. And if he didn't make the Olympic team, what then? One thing was certain—he wasn't going to work for his father. He hated his father's methods. Winning was everything to him, no matter what it cost the horses. For Parker the horses always came first.

Parker bent his head low, frowning in concentration as he dug out some mud lodged in the bridle's braided noseband. But he hadn't put Foxy first this morning, he thought.

Lyssa's words came back to him: "Have you seen the way he handles that mare? I've ridden her, and she's talented, but she's a handful. Parker has a gift."

If only he could be as sure of himself as Lyssa was.

It had been much simpler when he was younger, Parker decided. Riding had come easily for him. When others had to struggle and really work at it, Parker found he was a natural. It was when he'd gotten Foxy that he began to see bigger possibilities. For the first time in his life he found something worth working for. And for a while he and Foxy were an unbeatable team. Now things were more complicated, and he seemed to be struggling more and more. It was all very depressing.

Lost in his gloomy thoughts, Parker didn't notice that Lyssa had opened the door. She cleared her throat noisily, and Parker turned around as she came into the tack room.

"I'm sorry I butted into your business with your parents and all," she blurted out. "They made me so angry, I couldn't help myself."

"I know what you mean," Parker said, half to himself. "I'm just sorry you had to hear any of that. I guess you probably figured out that we don't get along too well."

"That's too bad."

Shrugging, Parker reached for another piece of bridle. "Thanks for sticking up for me, anyway."

Lyssa snatched up a sponge, sat on the bench across from Parker, and started cleaning one of his stirrup leathers.

"The first time I took apart an English bridle, it took practically forever to put it back together again," Lyssa commented.

Parker nodded. "I know what you mean. I guess cleaning off a loop of wire is much easier."

Lyssa laughed. "I know you don't approve of me

riding without tack—or any of my methods, for that matter."

"I didn't say that," Parker protested.

"You didn't have to. Don't you think I can tell? I can see it in your eyes."

Parker was silent for a moment. "So how come you're on your own here? Where's your trainer? And your parents?"

Lyssa looked out the window for a moment. "Uncle Cal's my trainer. My dad has been sick, and my mom and my uncle run things. Uncle Cal wasn't happy about not being able to train me for Deer Springs, but when he found out I could work with Sam, he perked right up. He's a big fan."

"You never really explained how you went from barrel racing to eventing." Parker commented.

Lyssa toyed with the fringe on her chaps. "Oh, I started to train Blue to be a roping horse. With all the cattle we have on the place, we can always use another working horse. But he was always bolting with me. He'd tear across the range and jump over fallen trees. I'd get thrown, and then I'd have to go find him. I decided I had to listen to him. He wanted to jump, so I had to learn to jump, too."

Parker smiled. "But how did you learn to ride the way you do now?" he persisted.

Lyssa didn't say anything for a moment. Finally

she looked up at him, her eyes almost scared looking. "Don't laugh, but we didn't have an English saddle on the place. So I had to learn to jump bareback. I fell off so many times, and all the ranch hands thought I was nuts. But eventually I figured out how to hold on. Then I started studying every book on combined training I could get my hands on, and I talked my uncle into trailering me to some of the local events. I was pretty surprised when we started to do well. Then I started traveling so much, I had to quit school."

"I heard about that—that you're home schooled," Parker said.

"People sure talk a lot," Lyssa observed. Then she went on. "Well, not exactly. I take correspondence classes. I bring my computer with me everywhere I go, and when I have questions, I just log on with my instructors and they answer them."

"Doesn't it get kind of lonely, not going to school?"

Lyssa nodded. "But I've made friends on the circuit, and anyway, I'm so busy, I don't have time to be lonely."

"But how'd your uncle know how to train you?" Parker countered. "Montana's not exactly—" He stopped short before he said something that might be taken the wrong way.

Lyssa grinned. "Oh, you easterners. You think you're the only ones who know how to ride. Actually, this old retired cavalry officer who lived practically next door came to our ranch and taught me so much. And Uncle Cal is a genius—he taught me to listen to horses."

"So you learned everything by reading and listening to some old cavalry guy and your uncle?"

Lyssa nodded.

Parker emitted a low whistle. "Sounds like a fairy tale."

Lyssa's face darkened. "Oh, it was anything but a fairy tale, let me tell you. I left out a couple of things."

"Like what?" Parker persisted.

Lyssa paused, but then she rushed on. "Well, a few years back my dad got thrown by a bronc, and he broke his back in a couple of places. He was in the hospital forever. The doctors said he'd never walk again, and with the hospital bills we almost lost the ranch. That's when my mom and I got the idea to invite guests and turn our home into a dude ranch.

"Mom had to learn how to cook for a hundred people at a time, and me and my uncle had to teach city people not to be afraid to get dirty. It sounds easy, but it was really hard. I used to stay awake all night, worrying. I'd think how selfish I was, trying to get to the Olympics when my parents were worried about losing their home. But then we started getting a reputation and the ranch started to make a profit. So, you see, it worked out."

"And your dad?"

Lyssa's face lit up. "He's walking again and even

riding some. Everyone says it's a miracle. But he lets the young hands break the broncs these days."

"You miss him, don't you?" Parker asked, searching her wistful face.

"Tons. But I promised my parents I'd bring home some Olympic metal one day. And I'm going to do it," she said determinedly.

"Yeah," Parker said. "I promised Foxy the same thing. But I'm beginning to have my doubts."

Lyssa's eyes met his. "What for? You can do it, you know," she said softly.

Parker pointed to his mud-caked saddle. "Oh, really?" he said skeptically.

"So you had a fall," she said. "You're a great rider. Everyone says so. I nearly fell out of my saddle when I found out I'd beaten you at Thorndale."

"I was kind of surprised myself," Parker replied. "I mean, you sort of came out of nowhere, and then you won!"

"Well, maybe I was a no name, but everyone knows you," Lyssa said. "I used to read about you in horse magazines, and I was dying to meet you."

Parker shook his head. It was too weird. "But then you met me and found out what a jerk I was, huh?"

Lyssa stood up. "I don't think you're a jerk. But you don't have to get so touchy when I say stuff to you. Sure, we might have to compete against each other, but that shouldn't make us enemies."

"We're not enemies," Parker said, surprising himself. Then a thought occurred to him. If they weren't enemies, what did that make them?

Parker regarded Lyssa for a moment. It was funny—a couple of weeks ago he'd considered the way she dressed to be strange and out of place. Now he found he'd grown accustomed to it. Actually, it was different and comfortable and, well, it was *Lyssa*.

"Why are you looking at me like that?" Lyssa demanded.

"L-Like what?" Parker stammered, and turned away.

"Oh, come on. Don't you get tired of always giving me a hard time? Think of all the energy you're wasting that you could put toward your riding." She held out her hand. "Friends?"

Parker was just about to take her hand to shake it, but suddenly he reached over and hugged her. "Friends," he said quietly, pulling her close. They stood for a moment, holding each other. Parker could feel Lyssa's heart beating.

They had just pulled back when Parker looked over Lyssa's shoulder to see Christina, standing in the doorway.

"Oh, excuse me," she said in a chilly voice. "I didn't mean to interrupt your romantic moment."

Then she spun on her heel and hurried away.

**10**

"HEY, WAIT UP!" PARKER CALLED, RUNNING AFTER CHRISTINA.

Christina didn't stop. "Save it, Parker. I don't want to hear anything you have to say," she called over her shoulder.

"C'mon, Chris," Parker insisted, following her. He put his hand on her shoulder, but she shrugged it off.

"Leave me alone," she said angrily, and strode away.

Parker stared after her for a moment, then he slumped against a pile of feed bags, a wave of resentment washing over him. Christina had no right to jump to conclusions and shut him out before he could get a chance to explain.

*Fine. I don't need her, anyway.*

"Yes, I do," he said to himself miserably. But then

Lyssa's face swam before him, and he felt his stomach churn. He had just started to like her, but now he was suddenly reminded of how badly she had messed up everything between him and Christina.

"Parker, is everything okay?" Lyssa asked when Parker swept into the tack room to gather his tack. He would take it home and clean it in the safety of his own room.

"No, everything is not okay," Parker snapped, pulling his bridle from the hook and hoisting his saddle on his arm. He turned and strode down the aisle toward his truck.

Lyssa ran after him. "You can't blame this on me," she shouted. "You're the one who's been ignoring Christina lately."

"Would you please mind your own business?" Parker shot back. "For once?"

Lyssa shot him a hurt look and then turned and walked away.

*Well, you've really done it now,* Parker thought. Mentally he ticked off the people who were mad at him. Lyssa, Christina, Sam, his parents, and probably Melanie, the minute she heard Christina's version of the story—to name a few.

As he drove from Whisperwood he toyed with the idea of driving to Whitebrook and waiting for Christina to come home. But then he dismissed the thought. He was so mixed up, he wasn't sure what he'd say. And anyway, he'd already been through enough humiliation for one day without having Ashleigh and Mike asking questions.

*Maybe Christina will cool off and call,* he decided later when he was putting together his bridle on his bedroom floor. Just thinking about it made him feel better. And when the phone rang, he smiled as he reached for it.

"Hi." It was Kevin.

"Hey," Parker said, barely masking his disappointment.

"Listen, I've been meaning to ask you. Next time you're on campus, could you pick up an admissions packet for me?" Kevin asked.

"Sure," Parker said wearily.

"You okay?" Kevin sounded concerned.

"Yeah," Parker answered. He couldn't face telling Parker what had happened. After all, Kevin had only just broken up with Melanie. He had enough on his mind.

"Well, I'm here if you need to talk," Kevin said before hanging up.

Parker finished cleaning and oiling his tack. Then he sat at his desk, thumbing through his USCTA Omnibus and rule book to kill time while he waited by the phone. It didn't ring. Finally he gave in and dialed Whitebrook's number. Melanie answered.

"Hey, Melanie, it's Parker," he said quickly. "Is Christina there?"

"Why do you care?" she snapped.

Parker frowned. "Put Christina on the phone, okay?" he pleaded.

"Say please," Melanie insisted.

"Stop being a jerk, Melanie," Parker said between his teeth. Nothing. "All right. Please?"

"From what I hear, you're the one who's a jerk," Melanie said.

Parker's face grew hot. "Could I please speak to Christina?"

"No, you can't. She's not here," Melanie said, and then she hung up.

An hour later Parker called again, but there was no answer, and finally he gave up.

After Parker had collapsed in bed that night and was reliving the upsetting events of the day, he found he couldn't get Christina's face out of his mind. The hurt and bewilderment in her eyes haunted him. If only she'd stopped and let him talk. She'd known him for years, and he'd always been honest with her. So why was she choosing to believe the worst of him? Throwing back the covers, he sat up and looked at the moonlight spilling through his window.

For once Parker wished Foxglove was at Townsend Acres instead of Whisperwood so he could slip down to her stall and just be with her. Horses were so much less complicated than people. For the thousandth time he regretted his decision to move back home to try to keep peace in the family. Some peace! He'd never been more at odds with his parents. They'd avoided him all evening, which was perfectly fine with Parker. He had enough on his mind.

When Parker finally slept, he had jarring dreams of riding Foxy over fences that got bigger and bigger as they got closer. Christina was standing on the galloping tracks, and he would head toward her only to see her vanish in a mist. The loudspeaker blared that he was off course, and the spectators doubled over in laughter. Off in the distance he saw Lyssa surrounded by photographers and reporters.

Parker awoke just before dawn, drenched with sweat. It took a few minutes for his head to clear and for him to realize that it had all been a dream, there was still a few days to go before Deer Springs.

And with deep certainty he knew that no matter how horribly things were going, he couldn't let Foxy down. Win or lose, he was going to do his best. And what's more, he wasn't going to sit around waiting for Christina to forgive him. He had to explain things to her, and if she was still angry, at least he'd have tried.

He glanced at the lighted dial on his clock. Six A.M. If he hurried, he could get over to Whitebrook and catch Christina out at the training barn. After taking a lightning-quick shower and pulling on his jeans and sweater, Parker tiptoed through the kitchen and out the back service door. Within minutes he was in his truck and roaring down the road toward Whitebrook.

Jumping from his truck as soon as he got to the stable yard, he made his way over to the training barn. He peered inside the dimly lit interior, where he saw several grooms mucking stalls and bustling about. Turning around, he headed to the training oval, where Naomi Traeger, one of Whitebrook's jockeys who often helped exercise the horses, was sliding off Just a Hunch, a gangly, two-year-old filly. Naomi's muddy goggles were perched up on her forehead. She handed the reins over to a groom and waved when she saw Parker.

Grinning widely at him, she called, "If you're looking for Christina, she's out on the track."

Parker thanked her and hurried to the rail, where Kevin was standing, watching the others breeze their horses. Kevin's jacket sleeve was pushed up and a white gauze bandage was wrapped around his forearm.

"What happened to you?" Parker asked, walking up beside him.

Kevin grimaced and wriggled his fingers sticking out from the bandage. "First ride this morning. I was a dork. I tried to talk to Melanie on the way to the track. Next thing I know, I'm flying over Second Term's head. He let me have it with one of his hooves, too. It would have made his daddy proud. Terminator's been dying to have a chunk out of me. I guess he sent his son to do the job."

"Bummer," Parker said. "You gotta watch out for those Terminator colts."

Kevin nodded. "Tell me about it. A little blood, but nothing's broken. Still, I don't think I'll be riding for a few days."

Parker's eyes swiveled back to the training oval. He could see Christina on Star, running counterclockwise on the track toward the red-and-white quarter pole. He watched as she turned for home and let Star open up, her hands kneading into Star's neck with each stride. She was at one with her horse, and he'd never seen Star look better. Overcome with admiration and guilt, Parker realized he'd been so caught up in his own problems, he hadn't kept up with Star's progress, or Christina's, for that matter.

He turned to Kevin. "Are things still looking good for the Derby?" he asked.

Kevin nodded. "Star's been turning in some great works lately. Cross your fingers."

Parker knew that racetracks were one of the most superstitious places on earth. He crossed his fingers, smiling weakly. It looked like Christina would be out on the track for a while longer, so he climbed up on the fence next to Kevin.

"So I guess you heard that Melanie's going out with that guy she went to homecoming with," Kevin said dully, his eyes not leaving the track.

"No, I hadn't. Well, the way things are going, it looks like Christina might start looking for someone else, too."

Kevin whirled around. "What?"

Parker kicked some mud off the toe of one boot. "We kind of had a misunderstanding, you might say. And she won't give me a chance to explain. That's why I'm here."

Kevin grinned ruefully. "I guess we're in the same boat."

"Oh, I wouldn't give up entirely," Parker said, remembering what Christina had said about Jeff not being interested in horses. He couldn't see horse-crazy Melanie hanging around him for long.

Star was approaching at a jog, and Parker climbed down from the rail, placing himself by the opening where Christina would have to come out. But she rode right past him, turning her back and handing Star to a groom. She mounted a fractious chestnut filly named Peacemaker, whom Melanie was ponying on Pirate, a blind ex-racehorse. Peacemaker leaped and bumped against Pirate, but her antics didn't faze him a bit.

"Settle down, you goof," Melanie said, her eyes darting over to where Kevin sat before she turned back to her work.

Parker could see Christina had her hands full. There was no point in trying to talk with her. His eyes followed her as she took Peacemaker out the track entrance.

Christina would probably work several more horses before she was done, and the morning would be half gone. With just a few days left until his date with the Olympics, he didn't have time to fool around. He had work to do.

All the way over to Whisperwood, Parker had imaginary conversations with Christina.

*I can't believe you made a big deal over one little hug, with Lyssa of all people!*

No, that wouldn't go over very well. It sounded too defensive.

*Chris, it wasn't the way it looked. It was just a friendship thing.*

That didn't sound right, either.

*Chris, sorry. I didn't mean anything by it.*

Nope. Now he sounded guilty.

As Parker pulled into the parking area at Whisperwood he smacked the steering wheel in frustration. No matter what he said, it would come out all wrong and

135

Christina wouldn't understand. It was useless to try. He'd better put Christina out of his mind and focus his attention back on Foxy if he didn't intend to make a fool out of himself at Deer Springs.

But first Parker had to set things to rights with Sam. As he groomed Foxy he rehearsed what he was going to say, trying to muster his courage. Apologies had never come easily to him.

Finally Parker was as ready as he'd ever be. Peering into the window of the barn office, he saw that Sam was at her desk, thumbing through her lesson schedules. Parker poked his head inside the door.

"Uh, Sam, got a second?" he asked tentatively. Maybe she wouldn't want to speak to him either after yesterday.

"Sure," she said.

Parker stepped inside and stood in front of her desk, feeling like a little kid. Well, he deserved it. He'd been acting like a little kid.

"I just wanted to apologize for losing my head yesterday," he said in a rush.

Sam sat back in her chair and regarded him. "You don't have to worry about me," she said. "It's Foxy you should apologize to. Going off and taking a fence when you were in such a huff. You could have really hurt her. You know that, though. I don't need to tell you."

Parker shook his head. "No, you don't. If anything had happened to her, I don't think I'd ever forgive myself. It wasn't like last time; this time I knew better—I just didn't stop myself."

"Lyssa really gets under your skin, doesn't she?" Sam asked.

"She did," Parker admitted. "But not anymore. We understand each other better now."

*But that doesn't mean I'm going to spend one more minute around her if I don't have to. She's caused me enough trouble.*

"Good," Sam said. "You're both talented, and if you made an effort to get along, you'd find you could both learn a lot from each other. Now, why don't you go warm up, and we'll get to work."

Parker smiled as he left the office and made his way to the tack room. He had a few days left to train, and Sam was going to help him. He pushed aside his worries about Christina. It was time to get focused.

A short while later he had Foxy groomed and ready to go. After he mounted, he settled into his long stirrups. Then he clucked to Foxy and made his way over to the dressage arena, where they warmed up, trotting figure eights and serpentines. Sam came down and stood at the letter *M*. She watched quietly as Parker circled.

"Foxy's falling inside," Sam said when he trotted

Foxy by her. "Do you know why?"

Parker nodded. "I'm not supporting her enough with my inside leg," he said mechanically.

"Don't just say the words. Really feel them and apply them as you ride," Sam replied. "And check to see that you're centered in your seat."

Parker went back to his circle. Biting his lip in concentration, he sat deep in the saddle, making sure he wasn't leaning slightly to one side or the other. Then he brought his inside leg to the girth and moved his outside leg slightly behind. This time when they made their circle, Foxy stayed rounded and balanced.

*Another small victory.*

Parker grinned more and more as the lesson went on. He was listening to Sam again, and things were falling into place. Foxy stayed supple and responsive. When she executed a perfect counter canter, Parker felt a tingle of excitement. He couldn't remember feeling this good about his riding.

"You know, I could almost start liking dressage," he said when the lesson was over.

"Well, good. It looks like you're starting to communicate again instead of forcing things." Sam smiled as she squinted up at him. "You can still use some more work, but I think you might be ready for Deer Springs soon."

Parker leaned over and stroked Foxglove's neck,

now darkened with sweat. "I hope you're right."

Sam waved at her next two students, who were mounting up outside the barn. She looked up at Parker. "Why don't you take her out for a trail ride and let her clear her head?"

After Parker had returned from the trail and had put Foxy away, he pulled his equipment list out of his pocket. Even though the event was still a few days off, he knew he had to start organizing everything he would need. After all these years he was still amazed at the number of things horse and rider needed to compete in a three day. Each phase required a special saddle, pad, bridle, and protective boots. In addition to feed there was stable equipment, grooming and braiding supplies, bandages, medical needs, horse blankets and a stud kit for cross-country. And that didn't even include all the changes of clothes a rider needed.

"I've got to remember to pick up my shadbelly at the dry cleaner," Parker muttered as he opened his tack trunk and began to sort through his equipment. He fumbled with a pair of rolled-up polo bandages and realized his hands were shaking.

Parker had forgotten the thrill he always felt when he had an event coming up. Deer Springs was the most important event of his life thus far. All of a sudden he felt very nervous—nervous and excited.

**11**

"TROT THIS LINE ONE LAST TIME, AND WE'LL CALL IT A DAY,"
Sam told Parker as he was finishing up his jumping
lesson on Wednesday.

"Sounds good." Parker clucked to Foxy, and she
moved out at a smart pace toward the huge red-and-
white vertical. The lesson had gone brilliantly, and
Parker was at least partly reassured that Foxy still
trusted him after his stupid move at the water jump.

But would she trust him in cross-country? Especially without Sam's soothing voice there to calm her?
He'd soon find out.

*There's nothing to be afraid of,* Parker kept telling
himself. But was there? Parker licked his dry lips and
rocked forward as Foxy tucked her legs and soared
over the fence. Then six strides and they were over the
next fence.

"Well done," Sam said. "I think you're as ready as you'll ever be." She looked closer at Parker. "Are you? You do have your test memorized, don't you?"

Parker swallowed nervously. "Yes, I'm ready," he said. He hoped he sounded like he meant it. Three-day eventing wasn't a sport for wimps, that was for sure.

After he put Foxy away and left her contentedly munching her dinner, Parker sat in the tack room and reviewed his equipment list one more time. *Guess this is it*, he thought as he drove away from Whisperwood that night. *Nothing more to do but get out there and show 'em what we've got.*

That night Parker knew there was no point in trying to sleep. He was so keyed up, he sat on his bed without bothering to change out of his clothes. Over and over in his head he ran through his dressage test. After a while he started flipping through back issues of *Practical Horseman*, only looking at the pictures. Then he studied his dresser mirror, where he had stuck several curling photos of Foxy at horse trials and events that they'd competed in over the past few months. They had shared a lot of good times together. Parker smiled to himself. *Whatever happened next, no one could ever take that away from them*, he thought.

Finally, just before dawn, Parker slept.

The next day Parker arrived at Whisperwood to load Foxy for the short drive to Deer Springs Horse Park. He had just finished hitching his trailer when Lyssa walked over to him. She twisted her thick braid around her fingers and cleared her throat several times.

"Uh, Parker, I hate to ask you, but do you think Blue and I could hitch a ride to Deer Springs with you? I think my truck has died once and for all. I tried everything, but it won't start," she said.

It took all of Parker's willpower not to groan. He needed to focus. The last thing he wanted to do was listen to Lyssa chatter away about *itancan*. And anyway, Blue hated trailers. If he started kicking out and upsetting Foxy . . .

"I'd like to, but didn't you tell me that Blue doesn't trailer too well?" Parker asked.

"I promise Blue will behave himself," Lyssa said, hurrying away to unload her equipment and squeeze it into Parker's truck.

Parker sighed as he loaded Foxy. To his surprise, Blue stepped into the trailer quietly and allowed the door to be latched behind him without any problems.

Parker looked over at Lyssa. "So why is he trailering so well today?" Lyssa smiled mysteriously, and Parker held up his hand. "Don't tell me. I ought to know by now. *Itancan*. But how come you didn't use it last time?"

Lyssa tilted her head. "It doesn't *always* work," she admitted.

Parker grinned as he climbed into the cab. At last he got the mighty Lyssa to admit her methods weren't foolproof. But then the next minute he wiped the smile from his face. None of this changed the fact that he was still angry at Lyssa for messing up his relationship with Christina. Good thing Deer Springs Horse Park was just outside Lexington, so the trip wouldn't take long. He turned up the radio as they pulled out onto the main road so they wouldn't have to talk. But the next instant Lyssa turned down the volume.

"Parker, I really appreciate your giving me a ride, but I still have to say something. You can't be mad at me about Christina," she said. "And don't tell me to butt out. I'm not butting in."

Parker's eyes didn't leave the road as he reached for the dial to turn up the music once more. Lyssa blocked his hand. "I'm not mad," he lied.

That appeared to satisfy Lyssa, and she turned up the radio, tapping her fingers on the window ledge while they drove the rest of the way without talking.

Parker's mouth went dry as he pulled into Deer Springs. The driveway was framed by elegant brick pillars and flanked by horse-shaped topiaries.

"Wow. They really go all out here," Lyssa said, her blue eyes huge.

"Never mind," Parker said, more to calm himself. "It's just another event." After parking the rig Parker and Lyssa checked in at the green-and-white-striped registration tent, where they received their exhibitors packets and maps.

"Yum. I smell eggs. You want anything?" Lyssa asked before taking off for the concession stand.

Parker shook his head. *How can she eat?* he wondered as he watched her go. But he was glad. At last he had a moment to himself.

All too soon it was time to have Foxy examined by the event veterinarians. As Parker expected, she passed the check with flying colors. Now they would be given their passport, which would admit them to the heavily quarantined stable area.

"We're on our way, girl," he murmured to her as he led her across the grassy grounds, which were starting to fill up with people. Ears pricked, Foxy flared her nostrils and danced, scooting sideways at the unfamiliar sights and sounds.

Parker was pleased to see that Foxy had been assigned a good stall near the end of the row and that the stall was bedded deeply with high-quality straw. After he settled her into her temporary quarters, he went back to the office to check his ride times.

He was thumbing through the glossy green-and-gold program, looking for Foxglove's name, when a cluster of reporters stopped him. "Parker Townsend, could you give us a few moments of your time?" asked a young woman.

When Parker nodded, she clipped a tiny black mike onto his sweater, then turned to the video camera that a bearded man was holding. "We're here at Deer Springs, where the triathlon of horse sports is about to begin. And with us now, Parker Townsend, one of eventing's bright young stars."

Parker felt his throat close. Normally having attention focused on him didn't faze him, but over the next few days there would be so much at stake. . . . *Stop it*, he commanded himself.

"Mr. Townsend, what do you think your chances are of winning this event?" the reporter asked.

Parker smiled easily, faking a confidence he didn't feel. "Well," he said. "Foxglove's been schooling brilliantly, and I expect her to go the distance. I'm pretty confident we'll have a shot at it."

*You liar.*

After the cameraman turned his camera to Dave Breen, who'd just passed by, a newspaper reporter thrust his spiral notebook in Parker's face.

"What about your chief competition, Lyssa Hynde? Do you think you can top her performance on that fantastic horse of hers?"

Parker held up his hand. "She's definitely one to watch, but all I'm going to say is wait and see." With that, he hurried away before anyone else could ask any more questions. It took a little effort not to run into other members of the media. They were on the show grounds in full force. Over by the souvenir stands he saw Lyssa being interviewed, and he turned quickly away.

Walking around the grounds for the next hour, Parker tried to steady himself. Finally it was time for the official walk, which was led by a former Olympic event official, who was wearing a blue blazer with the Deer Springs insignia on the pocket.

As he started over the course Parker dropped back behind the other riders, trying to shut out the sound of the official's voice. Usually it was good to listen to someone else the first time around, but Parker wanted to absorb the obstacles he was seeing without someone else's interpretation. Later, when he walked the course with Sam, he'd listen carefully.

*Talk about terrifying.* Parker swallowed hard as they neared the end of the course. He looked up and saw Lyssa walking off the distance at the Sleepy Hollow, a coffin-type fence with post and rail, followed by a ditch, and then a final element on a right turn. She was shaking her head and counting on her fingers. When she saw Parker studying her, she smiled and walked over to him.

"Don't these jumps look like fun?" she asked conversationally.

*She's trying to rattle me*, Parker thought. *She saw I looked worried and wants me to think she thinks these fences are no big deal.*

Parker glanced at his watch. "Excuse me, I've got to go meet Sam."

Lyssa put her hands on her hips. "Fine. So we were friends the other day and today we're not?"

"We're competitors today, and I'm going to give you a run for your money," Parker said coolly. "See you."

It was only afterward that he wondered why being so mean to Lyssa had become such a habit with him.

Frowning, he scanned the grounds. Where was Sam? He hoped she would make it in time to walk the course again with him. Just as he was about to give up and walk by himself Parker saw Sam's truck pull up at the guard gate. Parker hurried over to meet her in the parking lot.

"Sorry I'm late," she said climbing out of the cab. "Tor's new colt managed to open his stall door. I can't figure out how. He's a little Houdini. Anyway, we were all out chasing him."

"Is everything okay?" Parker asked.

Sam nodded and took the map from Parker as they walked over to the cross-country course. "The rumor is that the course designers had a field day with this one," she said, scanning the illustrations of the jumps.

Parker shoved his hands into his pockets and shrugged. "Yeah, I saw. But hey, Foxy and I can handle it."

Sam smiled and turned back to the brochure. "And don't forget the new penalty system is going to affect your strategy. Time is more important than any other penalty."

Parker nodded. He'd been considering the short-cuts he might be able to take over the course. Course designers usually presented several options at each fence. Riders could choose one approach to an obstacle that saved time or another that might be less tricky but cost precious seconds.

"You have to think about your short and long routes more carefully than ever before," Sam added.

"Short routes," Parker said decisively. "Don't worry. Foxy and I won't wipe out."

"Parker, I already know you're brave and coura-geous. The thing is, this event will test whether you've got the technique and skill to go with it. I trust you'll make the right decisions."

"Don't worry about me," Parker said, his attention already focused on the first fence on the course, a big, inviting oxer planted out with brightly colored flowers that spelled DEER SPRINGS.

"This one's designed to settle both horse and rider," Sam said, and they continued on to the next, an imposing wide jump consisting of two pickup trucks parked back to back. Sam frowned. "This is pretty unusual for so early in the course."

They walked on, discussing the various points of the combinations, footbridges, walls, and hayracks. After a while Parker's mind was a jumble of instructions. "Ride on the buckle to here, then gather up the reins to make the push to the brush." "Press down on the accelerator here." "Be ready for the turn here." "You have two options here: corner to corner to vertical, or vertical to vertical to corner."

"There, you got all that?" Sam asked, peering anxiously at Parker when they'd finished.

"Right here," Parker said, grinning weakly and pointing to his head.

*You're such a faker,* he told himself.

Sam didn't look convinced, but she went off to take Lyssa through the course, and Parker returned to Foxy's stall. He clipped on her lead rope and led her around the grounds to familiarize her with the sights and sounds. Before long a small crowd of kids had gathered around her, and Foxy surprised Parker by nuzzling one of the little girls.

"Hi, guys," Parker said, his spirits lifting at the sight of Foxy basking in the attention of her fans.

"I just know you're gonna win, Foxglove," crooned the little girl, who was gingerly patting Foxy's nose.

"Ooh, it's Parker Townsend," said another girl.

Two young boys rushed up to him, holding out their programs. "Can we have your autograph, please?" The small girl, who thrust her program on top of theirs, instantly crowded them out. "I was here first. Sign mine, please."

"Take it easy, guys," Parker said, reaching for a pen. He still couldn't get over how many young riders were into eventing, that they knew who he was.

When the swarm of kids headed off, Parker led Foxy back to her stall. He removed her halter and reached under her jaw to scratch her. She stretched out her lips appreciatively and closed her eyes. Her ears flicked forward as she heard the sound of someone approaching.

Parker realized he'd almost forgotten that he had to take Lyssa back to Whisperwood.

She reached out her hand to rub Foxy's white star, then turned to Parker.

"I just wanted to let you know that I've got a ride home tonight, so you don't have to take me. And Tor managed to resurrect my truck from the dead somehow, so I can drive myself tomorrow."

"That's great," Parker said. Then he caught himself. "That Tor was able to fix your truck, I mean."

Lyssa gave him a wistful smile to show she wasn't fooled. "Well, see ya." And she took off.

"Sleep well," Parker said to Foxy as he went to leave for the evening. "Tomorrow's a big day."

Parker was up before dawn the next morning. Thank goodness Kevin had volunteered to braid and groom Foxy for him. It gave him time to get ready and make sure his turnout was perfect. Carefully he put on his white breeches and starched white shirt. Then he tied his snowy white stock and slipped a sweatshirt and jeans on over his outfit so that he wouldn't get it dirty before his test. Carrying his polished boots, top hat, and shadbelly coat in a garment bag, he tiptoed down to the kitchen, where he intended to grab an apple and toast before he took off.

Too late, he saw that his mother and father were up and seated at the table and that Connie had laid out a huge breakfast. Parker froze in the doorway, his eyes resting on the back door.

"Surely you're not going to ride against those *Olympians* without putting something in your stomach," Brad said.

Parker winced at the way he emphasized *Olympians*, implying that Parker wasn't one of them.

"Thanks for your concern," Parker said, trying to steady his voice as he reached for an apple.

"Don't be ridiculous, Parker," his mother said sweetly. "Of course we're concerned. And we're going to come watch you, too."

"Well, I hope I don't embarrass you," Parker said, taking a huge bite out of his apple.

"You'll do your best, I'm sure," Brad said, and Parker paused in midswallow, unsure of how to take his father's comment.

"Yeah, well, I'd better go," he said finally, and darted out the door. Connie followed, thrusting something wrapped in a napkin into his hands.

"Good luck, Parker," she said, squeezing his elbow.

Parker thanked her and hopped into his truck. Taking a deep whiff of the hot cranberry muffins Connie had packed for him, he felt his stomach rebel. He pushed them away and drove on.

Half an hour later Parker had peeled off his jeans and put on his hat and shadbelly. Beside him Foxy stood ready, her dark coat shimmering in the morning sun, her braids perfect.

"I owe you one, buddy," Parker said to Kevin as he admired Foxglove's impeccable turnout.

Kevin grinned happily. "Get out there and ace that

test," he said, patting Foxy on the neck as Parker mounted. When Parker was aboard, Kevin polished his boots with a rag. "I'll touch you up again just before you go in."

Parker rode off toward the warm-up area. He had just ridden in the gate when he saw Lyssa at the far end, finishing up some circles at the trot. Parker stayed on the other end, warming up Foxy, but he couldn't resist glancing over at Lyssa. Even from a distance Parker could see that she was composed. It irritated him that she could be so calm just before such a big moment. He rode over to where she was adjusting her stirrup.

"Hey, you all set?" he asked.

"Yeah," she said, slipping her polished boot back into her iron. "Well, good luck. I'd better go. I'm on deck."

"I ride right after you," Parker said, preparing to ride off.

"Parker, I'm sooo nervous," Lyssa said suddenly.

Parker nearly fell out of his saddle. Had he heard right? Miss-Sure-of-Herself was having an attack of nerves? That was certainly something new.

He wanted to reach over and pat her knee reassuringly, but the last time he'd touched her, he'd set off World War III with Christina. Instead he swung Foxy away without saying anything and nearly bumped into another horse standing next to them. Foxy didn't like being so close to other horses, and she pinned her ears.

"A jerk to the finish, huh?" Lyssa snapped. Then she rode off toward the arena.

"Wait—" Parker shook his head as she started her canter. He hadn't meant it this time. Would he never get anything right?

"Number fifty-four on deck," came the announcer's voice. *That's me. Forget about her. You're about to go on,* Parker told himself. But he stationed himself near the entrance where he could watch Lyssa's test.

The stands were quiet as the flea-bitten gray entered the arena. Lyssa saluted the judges in their green wooden booth festooned with bunting and started down the line. It was during her first circle that Parker saw Soldier Blue's tail swish slightly. He shook his head, knowing that the judges would see it as a sign that Blue was resisting. Was Lyssa tensing up on his mouth? Was the pressure finally getting to her?

Parker's eyes stayed glued to the arena as Lyssa cued Blue for the medium walk. The gray had just picked up a comfortable stride when suddenly he broke into a nervous jog. What's more, it didn't appear to Parker that Lyssa was doing anything about it. Blue jogged for a few steps before he returned to the walk. Parker knew that the judges would mark the pair down. *How had that happened?* Parker had no idea. It wasn't like Lyssa to make such a basic mistake and override an already tense horse, causing him to break stride.

She finished the rest of her test without incident, but Parker felt a wave of guilt sweep over him as she saluted and rode out of the ring. Maybe he was the one who'd thrown her off. After all, he'd been a jerk to her seconds before she'd entered the arena.

"That was number fifty-three, Soldier Blue, owned by Black Thunder ranch and ridden by Lyssa Hynde. Now we have number fifty-four, Foxglove, owned and ridden by Parker Townsend."

There was no time to think. Parker entered at the letter *A* just after the bell sounded and cantered up the middle line, where he halted squarely, taking off his top hat in a salute to the judges. At their nod he started his test.

Immediately he could feel Foxy playing to the crowd. She flashed fire and brilliance as she made flawless transitions. Her circles were perfectly balanced.

*She's never gone better,* Parker exulted as they changed rein. But suddenly, without his meaning to, Parker's mind flashed to Lyssa's performance. It wasn't fair. He and Foxy had been the ones having the dressage problems all along. And Lyssa and Blue had been doing so well—until now, when he'd messed things up for her. She'd come too far to have one little mistake wreck things for her.

Now it was time for a flying change at the letter *S*. Parker suddenly looked out at the area where Lyssa was walking Blue and watching. For a second his eyes locked with hers before he abruptly shifted his attention back to what he was doing.

Several steps too late, Parker shifted his weight to give Foxy the signal to change her lead. She responded immediately, but Parker knew that the judges had to have seen that they were past the letter. He finished the rest of the test perfectly.

After he left the arena the crowd clapped noisily.

"Good girl, Foxy," he said, leaning down to pat Foxy's damp withers.

Lyssa rode up on Blue, her face like a thundercloud.

"Parker Townsend, what was that?" she demanded.

"Meaning what?"

"Don't give me 'what.' You know you messed up on that flying change, and I want to know why."

"Why is it that you're always pointing out my mistakes to me?' he asked, trying to make it sound like a joke. "So I made a mistake. If you think I'm thrilled about it, you're wrong."

Lyssa pulled off her white gloves and jammed

them angrily in her pockets. "You made a mistake, all right. But your mistake was letting down your horse—on purpose, I might add. And as far as I'm concerned, that's totally unforgivable!"

Parker was about to open his mouth when he realized that she was right. It wouldn't have mattered if he'd messed up honestly. But to let a horse down deliberately because he wasn't paying attention—it was the worst thing a horseman could do.

**12**

"SIXTY-EIGHT—PRETTY GOOD, PARKER," SAM SAID. SHE, Parker, and Lyssa were studying the penalty points posted on the electronic board.

Parker was disappointed. Even with his late transition, he'd hoped his dressage score would be higher. The dressage phase wasn't finished yet, and already five other riders had fewer penalty points. Still, Parker thought, straightening himself up, there was a long way to go. Winning wasn't out of the question. Parker's eyes flicked to Lyssa's name.

"I only managed a seventy, but I guess considering my stupid mistake . . ." Lyssa's voice trailed off.

"I don't want either of you psyching yourself out," warned Sam. "You've still got roads and tracks and cross-country and stadium. There will be plenty of opportunities to make up for any lost ground. Now, go home, both of you, and get some rest."

"You two look like a cover for *USTCA News*," Kevin said the next morning. "Definitely Olympic material." Parker had just put on his yellow jersey and was now fastening his black safety vest over it. His brightly colored helmet matched the color of Foxglove's leg wraps, and her glossy deep bay coat shimmered from Kevin's careful grooming.

"Well, we feel great, and that's what really counts," Parker replied. He was surprised. After tossing and turning all night thinking about his dressage score, he'd expected to wake up feeling anxious and irritable. Instead he felt pumped and ready for anything. Even the weather was cooperating—it was sunny and warm.

*Perfect for cross-country*, Parker thought as he fastened his armband containing his medical information and adjusted his pinny. Very soon he and Foxy would set off for phase A, the roads-and-tracks phase of the event, where Foxy's fitness and conditioning would be tested.

Kevin had carefully fastened the studs in the mare's shoes so that she would have better traction over the demanding course. Now he checked them again before handing the reins to Parker and giving him a leg up.

"You've got a whole cheering section here," Kevin said. "I've already seen a ton of Sam's students roaming around. Even some of your parents' friends stopped by while you were changing. And Melanie was here, but she said she wanted to get a good seat by the water jump."

*Did you see Christina?* Parker wanted to ask as he mounted Foxy, but he didn't want to hear the answer.

Shaking his head to clear his brain, Parker headed toward the starting area.

"Let her rip," Kevin called.

"Pace yourselves," Sam called, frowning meaningfully at Kevin as she came over to see Parker off. "You need to loosen her up before the steeplechase, and you've got approximately six miles to do it."

"Don't worry, Sam," Parker said, grinning at his instructor. "I'm not about to do anything crazy."

"Hmmm. We'll see," Sam said skeptically.

And they were off, down the road, covering mile after mile of rolling terrain. All the while Parker kept an eye out for any signs that Foxy was flagging or showing any stress. So far, so good.

And then came the steeplechase.

At the sound of the electronic signal Parker and Foxy flew down the track at a full gallop, flying over

160

the twelve jumps that were designed to test the horse's stamina and ability to tackle fences at racing speed. Parker's body instinctively assumed a perfect forward position. This was one of those moments he was glad he came from a racing family. Having practically grown up on racehorses had always given him a huge edge at this phase of the competition.

Parker knew that some riders complained about steeplechasing and had petitioned the USCTA board to get rid of it. But Parker considered it one of the best parts of eventing, second only to the cross-country. As he hurtled each jump he felt his adrenaline pumping and his heart singing. Because she was going so fast, Foxy jumped lower and flatter than she would over cross-country fences but always with room to spare. At the final brush Foxy gathered herself and sailed up and over. Parker wanted to shout to the sky in triumph as he galloped toward the finish line. Instead he crouched low over Foxy's withers and told her what an incredible horse she was, over and over.

Then it was on to roads and tracks, phase C. Still more grueling miles over varying terrain. Parker could tell that Foxy was bursting with energy and could go on practically forever. He could hear the spectators cheering them on, but he looked straight ahead.

Finally they reached the finish line, and only then did Parker allow himself to look out at the huge crowd gathered to cheer on the horse and rider teams. With a slight pang he realized that there was no way Christina would have come to watch him ride. She'd probably never talk to him again.

"Way to go, Parker!" he heard voices shouting. He was momentarily blinded by flashing cameras.

"You haven't seen anything yet," he shouted, pushing away his depressing thoughts as he headed for the ten-minute vet inspection.

Soon he and Foxglove were in the starting box, awaiting the countdown for the cross-country phase.

"Seven, six, five," the starter's voice counted down as Parker turned Foxy's back to the opening. He felt like he was sitting on a keg of dynamite poised to explode at any second.

*Now's my chance to make it up to Foxy for letting her down in dressage,* he thought.

At the signal Foxy shot out of the box and galloped toward the first fence. Parker rocked forward in his saddle, his eyes focused ahead. He had mentally ridden this course so many times in the last few hours, he could do it in his sleep. Foxy was moving forward eagerly with no sign that she'd already galloped for miles, and she took the first fence with ease. From there the pair made a slight turn and went up a gradual incline toward the pickup trucks, which the designers called the Truck Stop.

*Course designers and their sick sense of humor,* Parker thought grimly. *Well, Foxy isn't going to stop here.* Still, he knew he had to ride accurately to this big, imposing obstacle, and soon they were up and over it. Then it was on to the first combination, which consisted of two log piles with a ditch in the middle of it.

Soon they approached the Picnic Area, an intimidating combination that a lesser horse than Foxy would definitely peek at. For a fleeting moment Parker wondered if Foxy would doubt her rider after all the stupid stunts he'd pulled. But Foxy leaped over the wide picnic table and jumped out the next jump, a very narrow toadstool-shaped fence, without hesitation.

*She trusts me!* Parker thought exultantly.

On and on they rocketed around the course, always taking the shorter, riskier routes—to the delight of the spectators, who clapped their approval and whistled at each fence.

Parker became gradually aware that sweat was trickling down the side of his temples, but he rode on determinedly. If he was going to win this event, he had to be fast. Without looking at his stopwatch, he knew he and Foxy were making good time. But now he'd have to be careful. The next fence, the Hayrack, involved a tight turn and a real temptation for a horse to run out. Foxy cut the corner just right and took the wide rack boldly.

There was a long gallop before the next fence. While other riders would have to use this part to make up time, Parker used the opportunity to let Foxy relax a little before gathering her up for the Green Gate Brush.

"Rhythm, rhythm," Parker chanted under his breath as they approached the intimidating fence.

They were up and over, with a slightly sticky landing on the other side. Foxy recovered herself immediately just in time for the Lake, a complicated water jump that required one hundred percent accuracy. The longer route was tempting, but—

Parker ignored the crowd that was swarming everywhere and made the instant decision to go the faster, straighter route. It was over the round top, a bounce that required the front feet to touch down and pick up again before the back feet had landed, then into a pool of water.

This was where confidence on the part of the horse came into play. Looking at the pool, a horse wouldn't be able to tell how deep it was, though it was only twelve inches. Parker knew now that Foxy still trusted him completely as she splashed into the pool, her feet sending up a spray.

"Good girl!" he whispered into the mare's ear as she scrambled up the jetty and over the next round top.

The crowd's applause almost deafened Parker, and he felt Foxy surge ahead with even more speed. Flecks of foam flew from Foxy's mouth as they headed for Sleepy Hollow, the coffin-type fence. This fence could tempt a less experienced horse to back off, but Foxy took it flawlessly.

On and on they went, negotiating each fence with speed and accuracy, demonstrating what an excellent team they made.

When Parker saw the finish line looming ahead of him, he felt an incredible rush of relief. Foxy seemed to be spurred on by the crowd's applause and fought as Parker closed his hands on the reins, trying to slow her to a canter and then a trot.

"You'd start this whole thing again if I'd let you," Parker said incredulously, sinking into the saddle to bring her back.

He slid off and started unbuckling her overgirth. Kevin and Sam rushed forward, and Sam began spraying Foxy's coat with a solution of water mixed with rubbing alcohol. She applied it in generous amounts to Foxy's neck and chest, places where Foxy's skin was thin, to cool down her body temperature. Kevin and Parker took off her tack and began rubbing down her legs.

"How did it go?" Sam asked while they worked.

"It was unbelievable! What a rush!" Parker said,

knowing he was grinning like an idiot.

Kevin smiled ruefully. "You scared me on a couple of fences that I saw."

"But I didn't take any chances," Parker said hotly.

"I know you didn't," Kevin said. "I mean I was scared by how amazing you looked."

Parker hugged Foxy proudly. "Look at her. She thinks she's pretty hot stuff. Did you see how she showed off for the crowd back there?"

Kevin nodded. "Now, hand her over, and I'll get her cooled down. You go watch some of the others."

Parker gave Foxy one last affectionate pat and set off with Sam to watch a few of the more demanding fences. They found a spot on a low knoll where they could see several fences below, including the Green Gate Brush.

A few minutes later Lyssa and Blue came into view. They were galloping through the grassy area leading to the Green Gate Brush. Like Parker and Foxy, Lyssa and Blue didn't appear to need to make up any time at this point, so Lyssa was giving Blue a chance to relax and gather himself for his next fence.

"How's she doing?" Parker asked Sam.

"I think they're having a great round," Sam said. "Which is more than I can say for some of the others. There've been several falls, and a few others have been eliminated already."

Parker headed over to the last fence so he could watch Lyssa finish. As Blue came up to the final obstacle, the Garden, which was a big oxer decorated with flowers, Parker could see Lyssa's face. She was grinning from ear to ear. Obviously she was having a good ride.

And sure enough, when Parker went up to check the boards where the scores were posted, he saw that Lyssa had the fewest penalty points so far, and he was right behind her. Still, Parker knew he'd have to jump with amazing accuracy in the show-jumping phase tomorrow to have even a hope of beating Lyssa.

He wasn't going to dwell on beating her, though. He knew what it had taken for her to overcome her lapse in dressage. A less courageous rider wouldn't have summoned the heart to go all out on the cross-country course after a disappointing dressage test.

"You haven't seen Christina around, have you?" Parker finally asked Kevin when he got back to the stable yard, where Kevin was preparing a warm bran mash for Foxy.

Kevin shook his head. "No, but your cheering contingent grew. Ashleigh and Mike, Clay, Tor, and the whole gang from Whisperwood."

"Cool," Parker said, although he was disappointed.

From across the field he saw his friends waving to

him. He waved back. They came over and surrounded him.

"Great ride," Ashleigh said, and Parker flushed with pleasure. It meant a lot to have a Derby winner and renowned horsewoman like Ashleigh pay him a compliment.

"Hey," whispered Kaitlin Boyce, pointing to an older man in a navy jacket who was watching Parker and jotting something on a clipboard. "Do you know that guy?"

Parker turned to look more closely at the insignia on his jacket, and his heart leaped to his throat. "Yeah, that's Jay MacLeod, the *chef d'equipe* for the U.S. Olympic team," he whispered.

"What's he doing? Why is he staring at you?" Kaitlin persisted.

Parker's eyes locked for a moment with Jay MacLeod's before the man nodded at Parker and walked on, disappearing into the crowd.

"I hope he was measuring me for a team jacket," Parker said, at once happy and more terrified than he'd ever been in his life.


It was another sleepless night for Parker as he tossed and turned and ran through the show-jumping course endlessly in his mind. True, the jumps were much less demanding than those of the cross-country course. But that was the danger. A horse that was tired from a day of endurance and solid obstacles taken at speed tended not to have much respect for the stadium jumps. Parker knew this was where obedience and intelligence on the part of the horse would really be tested.

Parker finally gave up trying to sleep, climbing into his truck and leaving Townsend Acres to go to the horse park well before dawn. He felt like he was the only person on earth as he pulled into the parking area and stepped out onto the darkened grounds, lit by soft vapor lights. A low fog had rolled in during the night, and the air was thick and damp. Parker threw on a battered corduroy jacket and presented his badge to the guards, who looked him over carefully before admitting him to the stable area. He walked quietly to Foxy's stall, taking in the sounds of horses moving about in their stalls, some already banging on their feed tubs, demanding to be fed. Parker waved to a couple of the night watchmen, who were patrolling the stable area.

When he got to Foxy's stall, he was surprised to see that she was lying down. She regarded him trustingly with her wise, deep brown eyes, and Parker caught his breath, marveling once again at how lucky he was to own such a magnificent creature.

"Win or lose today, Foxy, you're still a champion,"

he said softly as he undid the latch and stepped inside her stall. Then he curled up next to his horse's warm shoulder and, for the first time in weeks, fell into a deep sleep.

He was awakened a short time later by the sounds of grooms coming down the aisles with their feed carts. Whinnies pierced the air. Parker groaned as he stood up, his muscles stiff and sore.

"Well, Foxy, thanks for letting me sleep in," he joked. Outside her stall, he bent and stretched, trying to restore circulation to his legs and arms.

After feeding his mare, he went over to the boards to check his times and once again review the course. Then he went to the concession stand and ordered a cup of hot chocolate and a bagel. Flipping through the program for the zillionth time, Parker eyed the bagel but made no move to touch it. He was so tightly strung, he doubted if he could even swallow. Several times he was tempted to go back and help Kevin groom, but he knew he'd transmit his jitters to his horse, and he was depending on her to be calm even if he wasn't.

A short while later Parker led Foxy over for the formal vet inspection and trotted her out for the ground jury. After Foxy was pronounced sound and able to proceed with the stadium-jumping phase, Parker took her back to Kevin, who was ready with a towel to dust her coat and hoof oil to shine her feet. Parker ducked into the dressing room in the front of his trailer and changed into his snowy white breeches, a black hunt coat, and his polished tall boots. He regarded himself in the mirror for a moment. It was amazing that he felt so churned up inside, yet he looked so calm and businesslike.

At seven-thirty the riders and their instructors walked the course. Parker, Lyssa, and Sam stood in front of each jump and discussed the difficulties involved with each one.

"It's nice how much effort the designers put into painting butterfly wings and catamaran sails on the standards," Lyssa observed.

"Each jump has a monster lurking in it, though," Sam said. "But neither of you has to worry. Your horses are in perfect form, and if both of you stay focused and remember your basics, you'll nail this course."

Parker was amazed at the number of spectators crowding around as he rode up to check in for his stadium-jumping round. They had jammed the stands and were standing in the aisles. Parker could even see that a few kids had climbed the trees next to the arena and were watching from their leafy perches.

His eye scanned the jumps, each one a riot of color and set off by masses of flowers, and he thought about what Sam had said about each jump concealing a secret. As he watched competitor after competitor knocking over poles and accumulating faults, he realized how true her words were. But then, he reminded himself, that was the point of the stadium phase—to scramble the placings and see which horse and rider team was truly champion material.

It always amazed Parker that even the big international riders who'd placed well so far found their dreams dashed over these seemingly straightforward jumps. First it was Cammie Dillon, who'd placed third at Burghley in England last year, who took down several rails and rode out of the arena, her sunglasses no doubt hiding tears of frustration.

Even jovial Oliver Flores, himself a veteran of a number of international three-day events, found his faults took him from fourth in the standings all the way to twelfth.

"Don't let these suckers deceive you," he said ruefully to Parker as he rode by.

Parker's mouth went dry, and he walked in circles, trying not to get too nervous to think straight.

As he and Foxy trotted into the arena a hush descended over the crowd.

"And now entering the ring, number fifty-four, Parker Townsend on Foxglove," came the announcer's voice.

Foxy snorted rhythmically as she made her first canter circle. The first fence was made up of fake brick posts and staggered rails. Parker tried to rock her back as he realized she was rushing, but Foxy shook her head slightly, as if to say, "Let me have my head." Parker made an instantaneous decision to do so, letting the reins out a bit, and Foxy ate up the distance and bounded over the fence with a mighty leap. She turned on a dime, cutting the corner and heading toward an oxer flanked by white bell towers. She took it at a long distance, and Parker felt himself nearly unseated, but he regained his balance as they headed for a tall picket fence, set on an angle. Parker felt his heart pounding as Foxy soared over it and landed neatly on the other side. Parker considered giving her a half halt but decided he didn't want to interfere with her momentum. He and Foxy leaped over an imposing combination, then negotiated a wide liverpool, then looped around to an airy vertical. Soon they were flying over a stone oxer and then a triple.

*One, two, three. No problem,* Parker thought as they landed after the triple and continued on to an upright plank. Suddenly Parker realized he felt like he was heading downhill.

*She's on the forehand,* Parker thought wildly, but there was no time to adjust. Foxy's hind leg rubbed the top plank, and Parker heard it drop.

"Five faults for Parker Townsend and Foxglove," said the announcer.

"Oh no," Parker muttered as his Olympic dreams went down the drain.

**13**

SHUTTING OUT THE GROANS OF THE CROWD, PARKER pressed on, knowing that he had to ride his next fence instead of worrying about the last one.

In one blinding moment Parker realized he didn't care about a little mistake, even if it had cost him a rail. It was the big picture that mattered. He relaxed and rode on, jumping the next post-and-rail fence perfectly. Then came the final line, an in and out. Foxy took it easily, jumping out roundly and shaking her head as Parker circled her to slow her. In spite of the five faults he'd racked up, Parker knew Foxglove had put in an incredible performance.

As soon as he left the arena he slid off and gave Foxy a big hug.

"Good girl," he said over and over. "I don't care

what happens. You were a star!"

Foxglove shook herself and nuzzled his pockets, more concerned with the prospect of a treat. Parker slipped her one of her favorite Polo mints, and she crunched happily as he led her around in circles to cool her, watching the other contestants.

Soon Lyssa was on deck, and Parker gave her a quick salute. She smiled tightly in return, looking nervous but pleased. As she entered the arena and crossed the starting line Parker watched intently. It was obvious that Soldier Blue was in fine form. His large, floppy ears flicked back and forth as he made his way over to the fake brick posts with the staggered rails. Lyssa leaned forward, her hands giving as Blue arced over the fence. He appeared to lope over to the bell-tower oxer, but he jumped it cleanly and squarely. Lyssa's face was a study of concentration as she guided Blue around the turn toward the picket fence. After landing on the other side Lyssa and Blue took the combination oxer to upright and put in the two strides between. From there they negotiated the liverpool and made the loop toward the next fence. Blue tucked his big feet up neatly and soared over it easily. Then they were at the triple. These fences had been the undoing of several other horses, but Blue took them nonchalantly, landing steadily and rocketing on to his next fences. His special blend of power and grace was unforgettable, and Parker could see the crowd was silently cheering on this unlikely girl from Montana and her comic-looking but awe-inspiring horse.

After Lyssa's final jump the crowd let out a shout of jubilation and stood up in the stands, whistling and clapping. The first clear round of the day! It was clear—Lyssa would win.

When the announcer announced Parker's second place, Parker felt a quiet joy seep through him. He and Lyssa exchanged glances, and he rode next to her as they stood in front of the judges' stand for the presentation.

"Congratulations," he called over the noise of the crowd. "I've learned so much from you," he added in a quieter voice.

Lyssa smiled. "Ah. So you finally admit it?"

Out of habit Parker glared and tried to think of a retort. But then he nodded. "So what?"

"Well, if it's any consolation," Lyssa said, "I managed to learn something from you, too."

"Like what?" Parker asked, puzzled.

"Remember when I watched you in the clearing while you were jumping?"

Parker frowned, then nodded.

"Those figure eights you jumped. I use those all the time now with Blue."

Parker sat up with a jolt. Of course. That was the

perfect exercise to keep a horse's weight back on its hindquarters when jumping! Lyssa had tried to show him how to achieve the same thing by barrel racing. Only he hadn't bothered to try it. She had taken a chance to try something new, and it had paid off.

"You deserved to win," Parker said, even though it took an effort to speak the words.

Just then Foxy reached over to give Blue a playful shove with her muzzle. Blue responded by dropping to one knee and bowing. The crowd laughed in delight as the cameras flashed away, capturing the moment.

"He never stops performing," said Lyssa, looking faintly embarrassed.

Parker felt a huge swell of emotion as he watched Lexington's mayor present Lyssa and Soldier Blue the coveted crystal horse trophy mounted on a gleaming wooden base. Then it was his turn as the mayor presented him with a slightly smaller version, in Parker's mind no less important.

"Miss Hynde, will you lead these riders in the victory gallop, please?" the mayor said.

Lyssa nodded and smiled. "Yes, sir."

As Parker followed her in the victory gallop, his red ribbon fluttering from Foxy's gleaming bridle, he knew he'd remember this moment forever. From here on in he'd keep learning and try his best because that was what counted.

"You did it, you did it!" Christina grasped Parker in a hug the moment he dismounted outside the arena. Parker's jaw dropped, and he felt suddenly shaky. He was grateful that Kevin was there to take Foxy's reins.

"You're here!" he said in amazement, holding Christina close and pulling off his hunt cap.

Christina took a step back. "Of course I am," she exclaimed. "Did you really think I would miss the single most important moment of your life?"

Parker looked searchingly into her hazel eyes. "Well, I wasn't really sure. I mean, after—after—well, you know."

"Oh, that."

" 'Oh, that'? Did 'that' have anything to do with you giving me the silent treatment and nearly driving me crazy?"

"Well, at first when I saw you hug Lyssa, I was mad and kind of jealous," Christina admitted. "But Lyssa gave me a big lecture about how I was being pig-headed, that the two of you had just decided not to be mortal enemies anymore. I still couldn't decide if I believed either one of you. But she kept pestering me, so I started avoiding both of you."

"Lyssa pestered you?" Parker asked.

Christina nodded. "Finally I decided neither of you was lying. I mean, you've always been totally honest with me. There was no reason to believe you'd changed overnight. But I knew you didn't need anything messing with your head before this event, so I stayed away, anyway."

"Oh." Parker almost sagged with relief. "Well, your being away did happen to mess with my head."

"I won't let it happen again," Christina said, and gave him another hug. "Uh, by the way, your parents are here," she added.

Parker shook his head. Trust them to turn up and dampen the most amazing day of his life.

"I heard them bragging to everyone that you were their son and that it was pretty certain that you'd be short-listed for the Olympics."

"Really?" Parker said in disbelief.

"Parker, Parker Townsend, this way, please. Over here," came a photographer's voice.

"*USCTA News*. Look this way, please," came a voice from another direction.

"Anyway, your public calls," Christina said jamming Parker's hunt cap back on his head.

"Your steed, sir," Kevin said, bowing jauntily.

Parker gave Kevin a playful shove and took Foxy's reins. "I guess they want pictures of the newest Olympic team horse," he said, rubbing the elegant mare's forehead. "Are you ready?"

KARLE DICKERSON grew up riding, reading, writing, and dreaming about horses. This is the third horse book she has written. She's shown in hunters and dressage, worked at a Thoroughbred breeding farm, and has been on cattle drives in Wyoming. She and her family used to own a horse ranch, and have always had numerous horses and ponies. The latest include two Thoroughbreds off the track named Cezanne and Earl Gray and a gray Welsh pony named Magpie.